RADIO SILENCE

DC MARRAKESH, BOOK FOUR

OPERATION MARRAKESH
BOOK 4

BLAZE WARD

KNOTTED ROAD PRESS

Radio Silence
Operation Marrakesh, Book 4
Blaze Ward
Copyright © 2024 Blaze Ward
All rights reserved
Published by Knotted Road Press
www.KnottedRoadPress.com

ISBN: 978-1-64470-502-5

Cover art:
ID 126123635 © Freestyleimages | Dreamstime.com

Cover and interior design copyright © 2024 Knotted Road Press

Reviews
It's true. Reviews help. Even a short one, such as, "Loved it!" So please consider reviewing this book (and all of the ones you've read) on your favorite retailer site.

Never miss a release!
If you'd like to be notified of new releases, sign up for my newsletter.

http://www.blazeward.com/newsletter/

Buy More!
Did you know that you can buy directly from the Knotted Road Press website?

https://www.knottedroadpress.com/shop/

ALSO BY BLAZE WARD

The Jessica Keller Chronicles

Auberon

Queen of the Pirates

Last of the Immortals

Goddess of War

Flight of the Blackbird

The Red Admiral

St. Legier

Winterhome

Petron

CS-405

Queen Anne's Revenge

Packmule

Persephone

First Centurion Kosnett

Encounter at Vilahana

Consensus at Aditi

Hegemony at Dalou

Princes at Ewin

Empire at Gloran

Domain at Yaumgan

Additional Alexandria Station Stories

The Story Road

Siren

Two Bottles of Wine With A War God

The Science Officer Series Season One

The Science Officer

The Mind Field

The Gilded Cage

The Pleasure Dome

The Doomsday Vault

The Last Flagship

The Hammerfield Gambit

The Hammerfield Payoff

The Bryce Connection

The Science Officer Series Season Two

Alien Seas

Buried Among the Stars

Captain Navarre

Last Stand

Lost Dreams

Ghost Towns

Games People Play

Prophet and Loss

Dandelion

Emergency

Warchild

Moot

Doomsday Girl

Princess

The Coven

Preacher Man

Captain Daring

Revoked

Returned

Reborn

The Lazarus Alliance

Escape

Return

Rebellion

Revolution

Liberation

Retribution

Alliance

Shadow of the Dominion

Longshot Hypothesis

Hard Bargain

Outermost

Dominion-427

Phoenix

Princess Rualoh

PRELUDE

Log: Directorate Cruiser, Tactical Transport
    Marrakesh (CTT)
Station: Horwin
Attached Special Mission Modules:
A+B) Forward Repair Depot (Double Pod)
Mission: Forward Survey and Rescue
Project: L72-S5R73V41
Security Clearance: 5+

1

Padraig studied the waiting room. His ship, *Marrakesh*, was again on Horwin, the capital world of the *Sovereign Collective Directorate of A'Zedi*.

He was back in the building that was was not part of the Ministry of War. As an *A'Zedi* sailor, and a captain to boot, he'd spent most of his adult life either in War Ministry offices or aboard warships. Today, he was in a place that he understood belonged to *A'Zedi Intelligence Services*. Nobody had to confirm nor deny for him now.

Padraig was in his best uniform, though he'd have stood out even in fatigues among the people coming into this building.

Civilians, almost every one of them.

Spies, though that rubric could be expanded to cover him now. He remained in uniform at all times, generally.

A'Zedi mulberry and mauve.

Today, he had hardly sat down on the hard wooden bench, alone in the waiting room with an older woman guarding the other side of the counter, when a door behind her opened and a second woman entered.

Mariami Gelashvili, Permanent First Secretary, *A'Zedi* Intelligence Operations.

"Captain Boru, could you join me, please?" the Secretary asked.

Padraig rocketed to his feet and was already walking. Across the large room with the hard, pitiless marble floor. Through a swinging half-door that was as good as a moat to keep people at bay. Through the far door and into a hallway.

He followed her to her office. Went to the seat on the right and stood waiting behind it.

Depending on how you wanted to view it, this woman was his boss. One of them, anyway. On paper, the Ministry of War still owned him. At least he thought so. It was hard to be sure.

He was merely a captain, in command of the last of the old M-boats still in service, the *Tactical Transport Marrakesh*.

What he did for Intelligence Operations probably made him a spy, anyway.

"Please, sit, Captain," she said, doing so. He followed suit.

The same desk he had come to know. Dark-stained oak from the look. Polished surface with a small name placard to remind you who she was, and a holder with a pen. No electronics visible. No art on the wall behind her or to either side.

Madame Gelashvili was a tall, heavy-set woman who looked to be in her mid-fifties. Hair dyed a golden-brown with reddish tones underneath, and hazel eyes, both of which were fairly rare in *A'Zedi*. Reasonably pale skin, compared to most of *A'Zedi*, as well.

Padraig's darker skin and black hair was the most common around here.

Gelashvili looked more like someone from the *United Technocracy of Wronlori*, which, he supposed, made a bit of sense, if she'd really been a spy when she was younger.

"I would have invited Squire Taggart to accompany you," Madame Gelashvili began without preamble. "But she is currently completing a training course off somewhere and will rendezvous with you on the ship. How quickly can you be ready to depart for a deep-space mission of indeterminate length, Captain?"

Padraig juggled numbers in his head quickly.

"We've just come off a refurb," he told her. "Depending on how long it takes to dock whatever modules you need loaded, we would need to transfer consumables aboard. And get Taggart aboard. Everybody else is under a recall order, so nobody has left the station where we're docked. I'm probably the last to board, having to travel the greatest distance, ma'am."

"Excellent," she nodded. "I'll put in a call when you leave here and get you moved to the top of the priority list for load-out."

That sort of power still left his mouth dry. That she could just call some Deputy Minister of War somewhere and *instruct* said person to act?

And they would. He'd seen it happen. *Jump*, and ask how high on the way up.

He'd done that, too.

"What's the mission, ma'am?" Padraig asked.

He might be a spy, but he was a sailor first and foremost. And he had a ship and crew that was going to cause a lot of his old classmates to start sending jealous hate mail one of these days.

And Intelligence Operations intended to send *Marrakesh* into harm's way.

As they should.

"I believe the term you would use is 'Search and Rescue,' Captain," she replied, nodding once to make a point of her seriousness. "The Patrol Cruiser *Northwind* was on a mission for us and failed to check in on time. They may have encountered enemy forces, but we would have expected some message, however bleak or abrupt, to be sent home via their Aetherial communications array, so the working assumption is that something happened to the ship itself, too quickly to say anything. You will go find them, find out what happened, and get them back safe if possible. Past that, I rely on your demonstrated ingenuity and professionalism to accomplish the task."

As in, *blank check because we trust you. Don't fuck it up.*

"Are you expecting us to tow *Northwind* home?" he asked.

Marrakesh was a tug, technically. They could do it, however slowly. If *Northwind* was on a mission for Intelligence Operations, it was probably in an unsafe system, surrounded by bad people.

"If necessary over the short term, Boru," she said. "*Marrakesh* will be fitted out with a Forward Repair Depot for this mission. A double pod designed, as I understand it, to telescope out during deployment, that various machinery can be brought to bear on a damaged ship, in order to effect the necessary repairs to get it as far as a proper base. That is already being moved into position for your Stevedore to load. You will depart this office to the roof where a transport will conduct you to the station overhead. You will complete load-out and depart without communicating to anyone outside the vessel except myself or my immediate staff. Questions?"

"Radio silence until we're successful, ma'am?" Padraig asked.

"At least the search part, Captain," she nodded. "Hopefully the rescue portions as well, though obviously you will be operating with much thinner guidelines at that point. I rely on you to continue to exercise the judgment that has gotten you and *Marrakesh* thus far."

She rose, so he did, stopping himself from saluting her.

Indoors, and a civilian to boot.

Still, Madam Gelashvili believed in him, and his crew. And had saved him from the sort of line command where nothing interesting ever happened save for the occasional battle, with him under the direct command of a Marshall of some sort and no chance for glory and adventure.

Sounded like this mission would have it in spades.

2

Chance Messier held the storefront while Padraig was down on the planet, meeting with his other set of bosses. Most of the crew was ignorant of what *Marrakesh* was up to these days, but she'd been brought in, at least partially, along with Kaitlin as Stevedore, so Chance understood what was up.

Plus, she'd been seconded to Intelligence Operations—though a desk job—while the kids had been infants, so Chance had a very good understanding of that side of the fleet. Nyssa Taggart could do things with computer systems Chance hadn't realized was possible. Ultrasmart young woman. Coming along nicely as an officer, even if she was still a year and change younger than even the next youngest Squire who had been assigned to the ship.

Sixth youngest crew member. Possibly the smartest, though Padraig had a lot of brains when you cornered him. And Chance did occasionally.

She smiled to herself and watched on the main bridge screen as a small tug maneuvered a huge office building slowly towards *Marrakesh*. Her comm chirped.

"Bridge. Messier."

"It's Kaitlin," the Stevedore replied. "I'm ready to shut down all local gravity systems while we dock our latest adventure."

"Understood, Kaitlin," Chance replied. "Stand by."

She cut the line and dialed a number.

"Engineering. Ahearn."

Knight Jareth Ahearn, Chief Engineer. The man whose job it was to keep the temperamental beasts aft tamed and pouring out all that power.

"Jareth, it's Chance," she said. "Kaitlin's ready, so sound the alert, then cut all of the Local Gravity Field Emitters, then stand by Damage Control parties in case anything happens with the pod."

"Understood," he said, a triple beep warning everyone that the moment had arrived. "Cutting in three, two, one, off."

The lights surged ever so slightly in response. Local Gravity Field Emitters required a lot of power, all the time, so those dedicated generators hardly ever got shut down.

Except when it came time to dock and undock pods. Then Kaitlin preferred most everything shut off, because some of them, like a Forward Repair Depot, were huge. And heavy.

Double pod, so it would slide into both sockets simultaneously, making this an even greater challenge, even in station with professionals. The thing was eight decks tall instead of the usual four to six. Came with a crew of experienced engineers already stationed aboard it and used to moving around.

Ships broke down. Even the best maintained ones.

Padraig liked to say that if you weren't using a ship up, you weren't doing your job. *Marrakesh* was old and worn, but they'd refurbished it fully out of the graveyard, then Padraig's new bosses had poured extra love and funds in, until *Marrakesh* was as good as any of the new P-boats being build.

Chance dialed the other line.

"Kaitlin, we're ready at this end," Chance told her. "Standing by."

3

―――――

Kaitlin had retired after her thirty years in purple. Wouldn't have come back, but for civilian pay rates and a captain like Padraig Boru. And a ship like *Marrakesh*.

The espionage stuff she was getting to do was really just frosting and a cherry at that point.

As Stevedore, she got to play with really big toys. Like, monstrous things, designed to slide into the back of *Marrakesh* like a sword fitting into a sheath. And with about as much leeway.

She was in a small shuttle, floating off to one side, like she did whenever she had to dock a double module. Singles were pretty easy to get in, if only because you lined it on four points and confirmed verticality, then dropped.

Doubles were more like dancing. Forward Repair Depots were even worse, because huge. One big tug instead of several little ones, because you had to handle offsets in the plugs, where you started off with less than forty centimeters of allowed variance, then tightened down from there.

The final adjustments were generally in millimeters, done with a hand-held impact hammer.

"Daneelson, it's Kaitlin," she said into the comm, talking to the guy piloting the big tug. "Corner three feels high. Adjust that down by about a degree as you slide in and lock. Proceed when ready."

"Yes, mother," he replied with as much sass as Kaitlin normally expected.

She chuckled with the comm off.

Most of these workers were young enough to be her kids, though she'd never had any. Didn't want them. Then or now. Got in the way of adventure, because she'd have wanted to stay home and spoil them.

Kaitlin watched the tug begin pushing. A LOT of mass there, but she wasn't in any hurry. They still had resupply tractors loading from the station side as fast as they could drive in, drop a pallet, and back out for the next one. Plus, Padraig would be a bit of time getting back to orbit.

And this was a job that needed patient strength.

Just because, she took the flitter's controls and shifted around some. Staying out of Daneelson's way, but seeing things from a slightly different angle.

"Daneelson, what's your read?" she asked as he slowly aimed both posts toward the sockets.

"System says I am on the beam but it feels a little wrong," he replied. "Oh, hey, that's perfect. Kaitlin, at some point, the pod's central spar has bowed outwards. Not by much, but I can't zero both bullseyes at once."

"How far off are you?" she asked.

It happened. Equipment got old and worn. Or a ship and pod built to the same expectations were outside tolerances when you lined both up.

Marrakesh was older than most of the crew, not counting her and a few folks. Even steel can warp like taffy, especially with some of the things she'd been aboard for.

"I'm ten centimeters average off both sides, when I line up the stereoscope," the man replied. "Suggestions?"

"Cut power and reverse engines to stationkeeping," she

ordered. It was her ship right now. "I want to check the underside."

"Standing by."

Kaitlin maneuvered her little hummingbird down to where the twin posts were about to enter their sockets. From here, she could see where the outer edges, fore and aft, were tilted ever so much out of true. Someone had bent the center of the pod at some point. Maybe the ship it had been docked to had flexed in battle or impact. Must have been a bitch getting it out again later, and they hadn't said anything to anyone.

Kaitlin made a note to look up the records of the last Stevedore responsible and send some friends in the War Ministry a note. A nastygram, as her old gran would have called it.

This should have been repaired before now, or listed in the log.

Still, she could make it work. The clamps that held the pod were heavy-duty. She'd just have to get it in, then manually adjust everything until the pod itself bowed back into true.

Good thing she had a whole team of repair nerds coming aboard with it, in case she broke something in the process.

"Daneelson, go ahead and slide it in, understanding that you can't get to zero here," Kaitlin ordered. "I'll fix it in the field."

"How?" he asked.

"Magic," Kaitlin replied.

4

Nyssa had always known she was smart. And had hidden it entirely after the first time she saw how the smarter kids were treated. If she'd been middle class or better as a child, it might not have been as bad, but her parents had been factory workers. Minimal education needed to operate presses and lathes, rather than designing things.

And the other kids in her classes had been vicious to anybody outside of the norm.

Thus, she'd played dumb, all through school, then got out and enlisted as soon as she could.

That might have been a mistake. Though, also, it might have been the smartest thing she ever did.

They'd put her through a set of tests. That had led to a second set of tests. Then a third. Then Radio School. Then more tests.

Because they'd started being nicer to her, the smarter they thought she was, instead of meaner.

Hell of a change.

Then they'd turned her into an officer. And assigned her to *Marrakesh*.

It had only gotten weirder after that. After *Sundering Wrath* and Monsanch. And Varfelis Station.

The last two weeks had been a deep immersion into cryptographic communications. The lead instructor—who had no name she'd been told—had warned her it would be a firehose.

Nyssa had handled it. Six hours of class and six hours of homework, every day. Blocks for sleeping, eating, and exercise.

Then back to the books.

This morning, they had come off schedule and pulled her out of a class where she and three others had been listening to a lecture.

"Mission assignment," had been whispered in her ear, and a homework datachip stuffed in her hand, before they handed her a bag with her uniforms and personal gear then put her on a shuttle crossing Horwin orbit from the station she'd been at.

Marrakesh gleamed in dock as her shuttle got close and she watched from the co-pilot's seat. Gas mining had polished a lot of wear and solar wind dulling from the hull, until the ship looked almost new.

With a giant gray turtle on her back. Obviously, something big was up.

Something on extremely short notice, too, because she was only supposed to be away for three more days. But Nyssa could see everything moving in ways that suggested the ship was hours from undocking, so her real bosses must have an emergency on their hands.

Something for Captain Boru. And possibly her, since she was training to become one of the top crypto people in the fleet. Or in *A'Zedi*.

Nyssa wasn't sure where she would end up. didn't really care right now, either. Anything was better than going home to the world she'd escaped from.

The shuttle came alongside the station and docked.

"They're too busy for me in the flight bay," her pilot said simply as he shut things down, so Nyssa grabbed her gear.

"Thanks for the lift," she called as she opened the hatch and stepped onto the station.

"Anytime, Squire," he called, but she was already in motion.

Across and down, to where the cargo doors were a hive of bodies in motion.

Maddox Nevin was holding a clipboard and checking things off as she approached. Armiger. *Marrakesh*'s Gunner, but obviously not needed in dock. Handling resupply today.

He looked up and smiled as she approached. Like her, a first-generation officer, but fourth generation sailor in his case. Cute, but more like another big brother, though not nearly the size or mass of the two she already had.

"Permission to come aboard?" she asked.

"Granted and welcome back," he said. "Something big brewing, because Captain got called to the surface unexpectedly and then they started loading us for supplies by knocking with the first tractor. Commander Messier has the bridge."

"I'll check with her and see where she needs me," Nyssa said, stepping past him and dancing around crew in the process of loading. And stuffing boxes into every available space where it could be held or strapped down.

Marrakesh had the two pod slots on her back, but not a lot of spare space inside otherwise. This much stuff suggested another long-term mission. Lack of a cargo pod filled with food and parts suggested something cryptic.

Like pulling her out of class three days early and putting her on a shuttle.

Forward and up, she found Commander Messier in the captain's chair, supervising several audio channels at once.

"Excellent," Messier said when Nyssa stepped onto the bridge. "Kaitlin Lynch is getting the modules docked but there are some issues there. Captain is in route. Resupply is ongoing. There is a packet for you by name, Taggart. Grab Halloran and start plotting our course out of here."

Whirlwind.

Commander Messier treated Nyssa like a much more senior officer, in spite of only being a squire, but the woman also knew a good deal of the extracurricular activities Nyssa had been assigned.

Nyssa saw Bex Magorian in the Radio station, so she stepped close when Commander Messier went back to what she was doing.

"Where's Zarah?" Nyssa asked her top assistant.

Nyssa was a small woman. Thin and compact, though average height, with her black hair buzzed daily to the absolute minimum regulations allowed.

Bex was *tiny*. And a pale strawberry blonde with freckles that looked more like a throwback to the *Enlightened Tyranny of Traisa* than someone from *A'Zedi*.

"Might be asleep by now, but I doubt it," Bex replied. "I spelled her about an hour ago. Lemme check. Security, do you know where Squire Halloran is?"

"Forward wardroom," came the reply a few moments later. "Late snack from the images on the screen."

They tracked those sorts of things.

"Good, I'll catch her there," Nyssa said. "Bex, you make sure that you and Coxswain Whelan are ready to move as soon as we know what and where."

"On it," Bex nodded.

Nyssa turned and headed back out, her duffel still slung on her shoulder because her cabin could wait for now. Or whatever office she ended up in, depending.

Zarah Halloran was the Helm officer.

Marrakesh was about to depart on a mission. Someplace secretive, from all the things rolling around her.

At least she had friends who would help.

5

———

Zarah still liked to joke that she was three days out of Uni, because her orders assigning her to *Marrakesh* had arrived on that third day. A year later, she felt like she fit in. Helped, seeing Nyssa Taggart enter the wardroom, that Nyssa was even younger.

Smarter, but not superior about it. Almost embarrassed at times, so Zarah had tried to be the older sister that it felt like Nyssa sometimes needed.

Marrakesh was a special place. Others she'd stayed in touch with let her know that. And were a little jealous.

From the look on Nyssa's face, Zarah started eating faster. It had been a quick bowl of fruit with fresh cream, because Zarah had taken one look at the sudden ramp up of activities and known that *Marrakesh* was breaking dock shortly.

Back to canned everything in a few days, enjoy it now.

"I've been on the ship seven minutes," Nyssa said as she plopped down across the table. "Commander Messier says that there is a message packet for me. Presumably secondary orders over what we're doing. She wanted me to grab you and start plotting our course out of dock."

Zarah nodded. Shoveled. Chewed.

Nyssa was a spy. Simple as that. And the spymasters loved her, which Zarah could understand, because the young woman could do things with your computer you didn't know it could do. Maybe it couldn't. And had.

But her glory would be enough to cover all of them. And Captain had quietly taken Zarah aside and let her know that the powers that be would take care of everyone.

"We got a surprise notice of loading," Zarah said around her last bite, then lifted the bowl and poured the cream directly into her mouth, sorry that she couldn't lick it clean. "Captain's day office?"

"Good a place as any," Nyssa said, rising.

Zarah grabbed her dishes and bussedt\ them, then out the door, heading aft in Nyssa's wake.

Taggart directed her to sit in Captain Boru's chair, then logged in. Then typed a long password into the screen when it came live. Like forty characters long. When the system already knew who she was, both the people and the computers.

Spy stuff.

A note from War Ministry, addressed to Captain Boru and Squire Taggart.

Zarah nearly swallowed her tongue when she saw the security rating.

5+?

There's a level above 5?

As an officer, Zarah knew she was cleared to 2 at a minimum. And maybe 3, depending on the mission.

5+?

She must have said something, because Nyssa smiled wryly at her.

"Obviously, you can't tell anyone, okay?"

"Well, yeah," Zarah managed. "Shit, though."

"I feel the same way, Zarah," Nyssa nodded. "Keep waiting for that moment I wake up back at my desk somewhere. In the middle of a pop quiz I haven't studied for."

Zarah laughed. Everybody had that nightmare. Usually minus clothes, for whatever that added to the terror.

"Here, your part," Nyssa said, moving down and highlighting that section.

Okay. Missing ship, overdue to report in and presumed in trouble.

Last known coordinates on the edge of *Wronlori* space, which made sense, because *A'Zedi* was at war with *Wronlori* again. Or still. Sneak attack at Eworn, almost four years ago, causing Fleet to bring back every mothballed ship that could fly.

Including an old M-boat Tactical Transport.

Mission to fly a specific arc, based on *Northwind*'s itinerary, dropping out routinely to look for signs of the ship. Or wreckage. Understand what happened. Provide repairs if necessary and possible. Return with intelligence and update the War Ministry.

"Okay, I've got what I need," Zarah said, mostly ignoring all the other bits.

Like how *Northwind* must be another spy ship. Same as *Marrakesh*, but a Patrol Cruiser instead of a Tactical Transport.

"You want to work here?" Nyssa asked.

"No," Zarah decided. "You'll need to brief the captain when he boards. I'll move to the bridge and start plotting things. What do you need from me?"

They were both Squires. The bottom rank of commissioned officer above Page, which was your training rank at Uni. And Nyssa was younger.

But this was a spy mission. And somebody had put Nyssa Taggart in charge of stuff with a 5+ rating.

Zarah could take direction from the woman.

"Captain's going to need a lot of depth on sailing directions," Nyssa said after a moment. "You start a mission-specific gazetteer with everything you or him might need while we look for *North-wind*. Route me any questions and I'll make sure that somebody loads up extra data if I don't have it buried somewhere in all this packet. How long until we're loaded?"

Around them, the entire hull bonged once, a long, low note like a church bell calling the faithful to service.

"That's the module docked," Zarah said unnecessarily. "Lynch will need time to zero it down where she wants it. Maddox has loading, so you should check with him, but I figure we're a minimum of four hours from now. Six feels like the outside window."

Nyssa nodded at her, eyes a thousand light-years away.

"Make sure you get a nap in there, but it might wait until we're under way, so you can digest everything and ask questions when I can still get you answers," she said.

"Excellent," Zarah said, standing and nodding. "I'm on it."

She moved to the hatch and out onto the bridge, shifting into her station next to Lead Magorian, and began calling up files to read.

6

Padraig knew it was silly, but the view of *Marrakesh*, sitting proudly in dock, filled his entire soul with light and warmth. He had always expected to make captain, but still it had been years early. And a Tactical Transport instead of a Line Cruiser, though they were the same basic hull design.

It was *his ship*. His first command. Possibly his last one, based on hints from Madame Gelashvili, but only because they might keep him there as long as they could, then promote him to Marshall when he was ready for a desk job.

Hell might freeze over first, but Padraig didn't tell anyone that. He was where he wanted to be. And had wanted since he was ten. He'd already seen more combat than a lot of Line Cruiser captains ever managed across their entire career.

Not a lot of folks in a better place than him.

"Message from the ship, sir," the pilot said, obviously listening on a headset. "Commander Messier wants us landing directly in the flight bay."

"As you bear," Padraig replied. The woman wasn't one of his. Wasn't even wearing a uniform, but that just marked who she really worked for.

As if Padraig had any doubts.

The shuttle sailed closer, climbing down and under a long strut holding the ship in place, then lining up with the bay door opening. *Flight of Fancy* and *Roadrunner* were both in place, shifted off to either side to make space in the middle. The runabout landed with a heavy clang indicating magnets in the gear.

"No gravity at present, Captain," the woman said unnecessarily. "Airlock tunnel is deploying for a soft seal."

"Thank you for a smooth ride," Padraig replied as he unbuckled and floated up and over his seat, then pulled himself into the tiny airlock closet aft.

The tunnel clanked outside, then shifted and locked. *Marrakesh* would seal up the bay and repressurize when they got under way, but this was the quick method.

When the lights turned green, he opened the hatch and kicked off, only needing to touch the wall once as he got to the main airlock and caught himself. Air Boss Walt Rafferty was standing there already, holding a stanchion and with a cargo crossbow in one hand, in case something had gone wrong. He smiled and closed them up.

"Retracting airlock now," Walt said. "Shuttle, you are clear to depart. Welcome aboard, sir."

"Glad to be here, Rafferty," Padraig told him. "Any change in status?"

"Overloading supplies, sir," Walt answered as they got things set, then he opened the inner hatch. "Squire Taggart came aboard about an hour ago. Module feels locked in tight. *Marrakesh* is gleaming and ready to sail."

"Good," Padraig nodded. "Keep me or Chance posted if anything changes, then be ready to break out as soon as we have clearance at our end."

"Aye, sir."

Padraig made his way forward delicately. No gravity meant you floated. And went in a straight line until you hit something or someone. He wasn't in that great of a hurry, as far as he knew.

"All hands, ATTENTION," Kaitlin Lynch's voice filled the corridor, along with a series of red lights suddenly blinking. "Gravity will be restored in sixty, SIX ZERO, seconds from MARK. Make sure you aren't under anything that might fall on you. Medical bay, stand by for the inevitable."

Padraig laughed to himself, then caught a staple in the wall and stopped, feet going down until they made contact. There was always somebody hurt when you did this, but *Marrakesh* did it far more frequently than most ships, so the crew was sharper. Instead of serious injuries, you'd get concussions and occasional broken bones.

Every light went solid red at ten seconds, then *down* returned.

"Damage Control teams, you are on for medical, then stand down and return to packing," Lynch ordered.

Padraig started walking. Chance would be forward, and Taggart was around here somewhere.

Then they'd count down to a mission.

7

―――――

Nyssa had read everything and digested it. Captain wouldn't have this depth of detail, so she'd be briefing him for the moment. Zarah had a course plotted and then had gone off duty to sleep. Cargo was being stored everywhere they could find space, if this was like previous missions.

At least *Marrakesh* had a series of empty cabins aft that the captain didn't let the crew overflow into. Those would be filled to capacity with cans of food. Life in the navy.

The hatch opened and Nyssa started to rise as Captain Boru stood there.

"No, you stay there," he said, waving her back. "Give me the ten-thousand-meter executive summary first."

He moved to the chair she usually sat in and settled, eyes expectant on her.

"*Northwind* is a spy ship," she replied simply. "A Patrol Cruiser configured for extremely long-term missions, sometimes measured in as much as a year at sea. They can run six months on internal supplies without any rationing. Intelligence Operations had them running a quiet survey course along the inner edges of *Wronlori* space, based on some of the materials we brought back with us from Varfelis. They failed to make check in when it had been expected, and there has been no emergency signal indicating any sort of problem."

"Whatever hit them, did so quickly," he replied. "Possibly disabling them. Maybe killing the ship."

"That's the general consensus, sir," Nyssa agreed. "We're equipped to repair things if we can. The orders include shifting our crew over to recover a derelict if possible. Otherwise, to recover as much information as possible, then make sure the ship does not fall into enemy hands."

His nod spoke volumes. As did the scowl on his face.

"How deep into *Wronlori* space did Fleet expect them to sail?" he asked.

Nyssa nodded. Double checked a map because that was how she did things. She looked up again and caught his eyes.

"There are suggestions in their original flight plan of a secret base not all that far from the border, sir," she said. "Data we recovered originally on our first mission to Albany, plus things that came up at Varfelis Station. *Northwind* was going to try to sneak up on it and have a peek, to see what was there, what kinds of defenses it might have, and if Fleet needed to do anything about it. I'm still not sure I understand how they could do that, though."

"Sneak?" he asked.

Nyssa nodded.

"There are things you can do to your Ghostdrives, Taggart," he replied with his own nod. "Shielding that reduces the signature on the Aetherial scanners. If you come in from a blind side, where nobody is paying attention, and move quietly, you might be able to get right on top of someone. Risky, but I presume that this vessel was specially built for such a thing."

"Patrol Cruiser," she told him. "Extreme long-range configuration, so stripped down to almost the minimum crew necessary."

"Yes. Fewer mouths to feed," he said. "And if something goes wrong, maybe not enough folks to fix things. Plus, if you are sitting dead in the middle of an enemy system, you don't necessarily want to broadcast your location. Those folks might be taken as prisoners of war, but they might also be arrested as spies."

Nyssa shivered at that. She'd seen a *Wronlori* spy captured at Albany, and everything that had happened to him.

"And a Forward Repair Depot?" she asked. "How would we able to fix them, if we're in the middle of a hostile system?"

"We're a tug, Squire," he smiled with that knowing grin that seemed to make it all better. "And we'll do what's necessary. You make sure that you have everything you need from the Fleet and the bosses before we break away, because we'll be operating in radio silence as soon as we undock from the station. Am I clear?"

"You are, sir," she said, watching him rise and move to the door without ever suggesting she vacate his office.

Then she was alone.

Nyssa started digging deeper into the files.

8

Padraig moved close to where Chance was in command, but like Taggart, waved her to remain seated.

"I'll let you handle getting us out of dock," he told her. "We've got a long run from here, and we'll be radio silent for much of it."

He watched her eyes for recognition of what that implied.

She'd worked for Fleet Intelligence before *Marrakesh*, so Chance Messier might be the best 2IC he could have asked for, given his new job.

"We're loading everything they can stuff in," Chance replied in a breezy voice that contained all sorts of extra things.

Like, how much could really be stuffed back there, if you were trying. But then, if something had happened to *Northwind*, they might be rationing food and hoping that someone like *Marrakesh* came riding over the hill in the nick of time to rescue them.

"How long until we're set?" he asked simply.

"Couple of hours," she answered. "Kaitlin is locking her stuff down. Maddox is in charge of packing and I've told him to load until the fire marshal issues him a ticket for safety violations aft. Everyone else has been recalled and accounted for. You are the last to board."

"Excellent," he smiled. "You stay on that. I'll head aft and check in with Kaitlin. Once we get clear and into Ghost-space, there will be a senior officer briefing with more details."

She nodded knowingly. Minister Gelashvili hadn't met her directly, but had authorized Padraig to share enough, and Chance was smart enough to fill in the gaps he'd left.

Padraig headed back to where Kaitlin Lynch would be working. Docking a double pod was always an adventure in three-dimensional puzzle solving, so she'd be working with her crews to get it in where she wanted. And something this big would take some effort.

He found her exactly where he expected, looming over Command Expert Den Gilroy's shoulder as he worked with a two-handed impact hammer as long as his arm. As Docker, it was his job, even as much as the Stevedore wanted to do it herself from the way she was rocking her weight back and forth as Padraig snuck up on them.

Surrounded by three strangers he didn't know, one male and two female, but almost every pod *Marrakesh* carried came with a permanent crew added on. Kaitlin's main job as Stevedore was to provide a human interface to those folks when they came aboard. And she was absolutely impressive at it.

The male, shorter than average and broad in the shoulders and chest. No uniform, which made him stand out, but he did have tabs on his collars indicating that he was *Civilian in Charge*. Always a good idea in situations like this, when he might need to overrule a Fleet Marshal on the readiness of their vessel.

Two women stood nearby, one a tall and skinny Commander and the other a perfectly average brunette Knight. Perfectly average until the brunette locked those bright blue eyes on him as he approached and Padraig watched all manner of instant calculations and assessments.

They shared a nod when she saw his rank tabs and Padraig slid in close to watch Gilroy as he grunted profanities at Kaitlin's varied suggestions.

Not quite an old married couple, but the relationship was similar in many ways, as they had to work that closely together constantly.

Finally, the impact hammer stopped thumping. Gilroy looked up and started when he saw his Captain smiling nearby. Kaitlin did the same. The others were more phlegmatic.

"Captain, we're about ready to go here," Docker Gilroy announced as he stood up. "A couple of tests to run, but we're dead centered on the beam. Somebody's getting yelled at later when we detach it, though."

"Oh?" Padraig asked.

The Civilian and the two women jolted at the familiarity, but Padraig had long since learned that a well-trained crew would have opinions on things and a smart commander listened.

Den nodded to Kaitlin, who grimaced.

"The bridge connecting the two sides flexed at some point," she explained. "Not bad enough to do anything but make docking a bit of a pain, but it should have been noted. We could have been ready an hour ago had it been true."

Padraig turned to the man, catching his grimace as well. Then a shrug.

"Walker Nylund," the man introduced himself as he held out a hand. "And she's probably correct, but I've also never been aboard a Tug with standards this high, Captain. Others hardly noticed and just crammed the pod into place by main force."

He was smiling, which was good. *Marrakesh* had been fully refurbished out of the boneyard, and then drydocked twice since, after missions that required full inspections.

And Kaitlin Lynch ran a tight shop.

"Padraig Boru," he replied. "I like to think that I have the best ship and crew in the fleet, Mr. Nylund. You've met some of them, but the rest are just as good. Your officers?"

"Commander Thalia Leath," he indicated the tall, skinny woman with ash blonde hair. "She's my Second-in-Command and EVA Boss when we're operational. Knight Jocelyn Konicek is my EVA expert and possibly third in the hierarchy around here."

Padraig shook hands with both women and smiled.

"Welcome aboard," he said brightly. "Commander Messier tells me that we are a few hours from departure, followed by a high-speed run to our destination. There will be a senior officer briefing after break-away, where we can get deeper into the details of what was something of an emergency mission, pulling all of us off our usual routines."

Nylund started to speak, then caught himself, noting the handful of enlisted sailors standing around, on call in case Gilroy or Kaitlin needed something done in a hurry. He nodded instead.

"We're pretty self-contained in the forward pod, Captain," Nylund said instead. "The three of us are probably the people you need to talk to, as, like you, this got dropped on us in a hurry."

Padraig checked a wall clock.

"Dinner will be in about five hours," he decided. "We'll eat, then retire to a conference room for our briefing. As usual, please let Kaitlin know if you need anything. Once we break away from the station, we'll be running hard and not stopping anywhere along the way if we forgot something. Questions?"

All three—five with Kaitlin and Den—shook their heads, so Padraig nodded and backed away.

"I will see you in a few hours, then," he announced before anyone asked any questions he didn't feel like answering right now.

He had an exceptional crew. A couple of sailors had been transferred off when Intelligence took over his life, presumably because they weren't considered entirely trustworthy for this sort of thing, but the rest had kept walking without missing a beat.

And he had a mission ahead that would test them like nothing had before.

9

––––––––––

Chance had been surprised that Padraig had left her in charge of the bridge, but equally pleased. His personal philosophy was that everyone should be trained to do their boss's job, and maybe a couple levels above that, so that they could step in regardless of the situation or circumstances if something happened.

This felt like his way of making sure she was ready for her own boat, one of these days. At the same time, Chance wasn't sure she wanted something like that, if it meant giving up everything that *Marrakesh* represented.

She'd been in Personnel for a stint, so she understood that someone had captured magic with this crew. Lightning in a bottle.

Anywhere else she went, even her own deck, would be a bit of a letdown.

So she was prepared to ride this gig as long and as far as she could.

Chance looked around her bridge, reveling in that feeling.

"Radio, what is your status?" she called.

Bex Magorian was handling communication duties today, mostly because Taggart was busy drinking from a firehose of data, trying to turn it into information for Padraig while they still had a hardline link to ask questions.

"All channels clear, Commander," Bex nodded. "Lane assignment transmitted."

Like Chance, trained up so she could handle it. Possibly a field commission, one of these days, if the woman desired. She was good. Not as good as Nyssa, but nobody else was.

Chance keyed a line aft.

"Engineering. Ahearn."

Chief Engineer, in charge of wrangling all the big generators, as well as the crew of goofballs and misfits who made them work. There were days Chance expected to walk into Engineering and find them in the middle of a Bollywood Dance Routine interlude, though she was careful never to suggest it if nobody else had put that idea in their heads.

Yet.

"Jareth, how are we for power?" Chance asked.

"All my trolls are purring, Commander," he replied.

"Don't care about the crew," she said with a smile. "What about the generators?"

Chance caught the laughter in the background, both here on the bridge as well as aft.

"One hundred percent ready to fly, sir," Jareth laughed.

Chance cut the line and dialed another.

"Stevedore," Kaitlin replied.

"You all locked down for flight?" Chance asked.

"Affirmative," Kaitlin replied. "Chatting with my new friends about how they might disassemble parts of the pod connector span to straighten it in flight."

"They can do that?" Chance gasped.

"*They* can," Kaitlin replied with a smile in her voice.

Chance was impressed. Usually, that was something you did in dock, with the pod separated and boomed to the station. Not docked, locked, and powered.

Walker Nylund must have almost as good a crew as she did, if he thought they could manage.

Chance nodded and turned to Zarah Halloran. Young like so many here, but growing into herself.

"Helm, stand by to unlock spars and detach for free flight," Chance ordered.

"All spars read green, Commander," Zarah replied with a firm nod.

Chance looked around for any last-minute surprises. Seeing none, she nodded to herself.

"Helm, undock us," she ordered.

Zarah's hands tapped three controls and the hull rang with bells and gongs as grapples detached and pulled away. It took nearly a minute, but that was planned as well, each one going in a specific sequence and confirming the one before it had released clean before acting.

Last thing you wanted was to be jerked sideways into the station itself and dent or tear something.

"Commander, *Marrakesh* is free," Zarah announced finally.

"Ahead two percent on current path," Chance ordered.

"All ahead two, aye."

Lots of mass, slow to accelerate, but the ship began oozing away from the retracting docking arms. Open space beckoned quickly.

"Radio, how is our flight corridor?" Chance called.

"Clear of all vessels, Commander," Bex replied.

"Helm, ahead six percent," Chance ordered. "Maintain clearance and heading."

"Six percent and true, aye," Zarah answered.

Chance nodded. Something big was coming. Padraig would have all the details in a while.

Felt like whatever it was, *Marrakesh* was riding to the rescue.

10

After two weeks in flight, Nyssa had fallen into a pattern with her research.

Intelligence had transmitted a tremendous amount of background material, but she read quickly and the captain had given her downtime so others could train while the ship was in FTL flight.

Right now was her off-duty time, so she was reading in a study room, instead of training, certifying, or preparing. This information was more important than that. At least today.

Forward Aetherial scanners listened passively for someone approaching on any sort of intercept course, while rear-facing ones made sure nobody snuck up on them.

The ship had been going much faster, closer to home, but as *Marrakesh* approached the frontier zones facing *Wronlori*, Captain Boru had progressively slowed down. Less signal being broadcast that a ship was in Ghost-space, so maybe nobody would notice them.

Plus, she and Zarah had plotted a course that wound up and over most of the inhabited zones. It helped that the galactic disk was thinly populated here, so they'd used that third dimension to hide in.

Nyssa checked the clock and realized that she'd been deeper than she'd realized. Closing the screen, she stood up and stretched, even as the comm beeped.

"Taggart," she said automatically, answering.

"We're getting close," Bex replied. "Captain wants you forward."

"Be there in ninety seconds," Nyssa said, cutting the line.

She could be there in fifteen if she sprinted, but there'd been no emergency alert, so hopefully they were merely coming up on a set of coordinates in the middle of nowhere.

The first spot where *Northwind* had settled in to scan the frontier before crossing it and slipping into *Wronlori* space.

Nothing important around here. Nearest solar system of any kind was more than four light-years away. Nearest known inhabited one was closer to ten.

Nyssa entered the bridge to Captain Boru's smile and nod, then slipped into her station and unlocked all the new functions she'd been promoted to. Zarah was flying. Maddox had command of the guns. Commander Messier and Bex would be aft in the secondary bridge like usual.

Not combat, but the air had that edge to it as she brought everything live and listened to the music of the aetherial sphere.

"Radio," Captain Boru called as she settled in. "Anything?"

"Negative, sir," she replied after confirming. "No manufactured signals in range. If anyone is present, they are hiding dark."

Always a risk. Especially when approaching via FTL. Someone could shut down all their active transmitters and wait like a trapdoor spider, pouncing once you got too close.

Marrakesh had hardly any firepower for a ship this size, but she could always run. During the latest dry-dock, they'd taken the time to tune everything, and a team of mechanics and engineers from the pod had had nothing better to do than practice maintenance duties on *Marrakesh* as the ship flew.

It felt cleaner and faster than it had, back freshly relaunched with this new crew a year and a half ago.

Nyssa studied all the places where her new training might have suggested putting a station or beacon to listen, knowing that they were almost close enough to the *Wronlori/A'Zedi* border to touch it.

Or rather, deep in a zone a few light-years across that both claimed and neither had put any effort into holding.

So far.

She checked the notes that Fleet had sent along, comparing them to her current location as triangulated by the five closest stars. Deep space, so margins of error were measured in light-minutes.

She drew a breath and listened to...something.

The Music of the Spheres?

Nyssa turned back to Captain Boru, noted that he was watching her.

"Permission to adjust our current location, sir?" she asked tentatively.

"Go ahead, Taggart," he replied immediately.

Nyssa looked at the plot. Thought about sneaking past here into the depths of *Wronlori* space, and how she might do it, based on the new training that nobody but her had been given.

How to think like *Northwind*'s captain.

"Helm, bring us down ten," Nyssa ordered. "Come to three-five-three and rotate forty degrees clockwise. Then ahead five percent."

Why those specific modifications, she couldn't have told anyone, save that it *felt* right.

"Down ten, three-five-three, forty, aye," Zarah replied, tapping on her keys. "Ahead five."

The stars had moved around, coming to rest before the ship started forward. Nyssa sent a quiet ping ahead of the ship. Hardly any power to the signal, so that nobody would pick it up at any range.

What she was looking for was close.

Minutes passed, and her board beeped.

Yes, there.

"What do you have, Radio?" Captain Boru asked quietly.

The whole bridge had gotten quiet, voices dropped almost to whispers.

"*Northwind* left a buoy, sir," Nyssa replied. "It responded to a specific signal from us, and would ignore anything else."

"Helm, plot an intercept course," the captain ordered. "Radio, how big is it?"

Nyssa studied her notes.

"Roughly the size of a probe, sir," she said. "Two meters long by about sixty centimeters across in a flattened lozenge shape."

"Can we recover it?" he asked.

"EVA, sir," she said. "Too small for a shuttle to dock, but it could pull alongside and grab it."

She looked back when he dialed a number.

"Stevedore," Ms. Lynch replied.

"Kaitlin, can you ask Mister Nylund if I can borrow Knight Konicek for an EVA?" he asked.

Oh. Of course. They had an EVA expert on hand.

"She's nodding at me, Padraig," Lynch replied.

"Taggart, send them back the data they need," he ordered.

"Flight Deck. Rafferty."

"I need *Flight of Fancy* warmed up for an EVA recovery operation, Chief," Captain Boru continued.

"Coming up."

Nyssa transmitted the data aft and settled in to watch some other experts go to work.

11

Padraig had brought Chance and Kaitlin, as usual, to hear Nyssa Taggart's briefing. Walker Nylund had brought Leath and Konicek, the latter in a bodysuit as close to out of uniform as you could get without crossing, but she'd only paused to strip her spacesuit off when she got back.

Padraig didn't particularly like women that way, but the way that outfit appeared painted on was something he found distracting. In a good way.

She caught him looking at one point and smiled. He blushed just a little. It had been at least five years since he'd actually gone to bed with a woman.

He settled himself and focused on Taggart's words.

"From there," she was saying, "they listened to several systems, then plotted a slightly different course to approach the target system of Domnall. Depending on what happened, we might have missed them, given our need to keep emissions to a minimum."

Padraig caught Nylund's scowl.

"Captain, what are your expectations?" the man asked bluntly.

"We're going in to see what we can find," Padraig replied

simply. "*Northwind* is long overdue to check in, and you understand what they were doing. I can't tell you more until we determine their status. My expectation is that I'll put as much of your crew aboard as we can when we find them, then you will tell me what it will take to get the crew home."

"And the ship?" Nylund pressed.

"Rescued if we can," Padraig said. "Destroyed if we must, to prevent it falling into enemy hands."

The three engineers grimaced, but he understood that they saw such a thing as a professional failing. They were repair experts. Move heaven and earth to fix a ship and get it back into battle.

Sometimes, though, you couldn't.

He turned back to Nyssa.

"You mentioned two other checkpoints?" he asked.

"Aye, sir," she nodded. "Both would likely be empty, unless something had happened to change their plans. My expectation is that they got to Domnall and something happened there."

"Agreed, but we have to balance speed with precision," he said. "You work with Halloran to plot a course that gets us to each as quickly as it's safe, but we'll only scan for wreckage or another buoy before moving on. You mentioned a different approach?"

"They'll come in higher and from about thirty degrees left, as seen from the star itself, sir," she nodded. "There is a new mining colony that they picked up along the previous flight path, so they were taking an extra precaution to evade it."

"Understood," he said. "You get in motion now and have Chance get us into Ghost-space as quickly as possible. Dismissed."

He watched her and Chance depart immediately. Kaitlin and Nylund rose and drifted into a technical discussion that drew Leath in as well, the three following Nyssa.

Padraig found himself alone with Konicek. Knight, so middle rank as an officer. Average-looking woman in many ways, with bright blue eyes and brown hair. Lots and lots of brains, he had discovered, which was perhaps what he found attractive about her, in spite of her gender.

"Should I be prepared to quickly EVA at the next two stops?" she asked.

It sounded innocent, but he caught the implications that she'd be wearing this outfit, with rank badge and logo *painted onto flesh*, it seemed.

Her grin gave her away.

"It might save time if we end up needing you outside the ship," he noted dryly, uncertain why he was flirting with the woman, except that he was.

Smart. Attractive enough in a regular sort of way. Lots of average that added up to something interesting, he supposed.

"And your crew won't mind me like this?" she gestured to herself, skin-tight mauve outlining and somehow emphasizing everything.

And he didn't normally like girls.

Still.

"They'll get over themselves," he noted.

Padraig rose from the table. He was tall. Konicek was average, so he had a head on her. Nyssa was perhaps the darkest around here, in terms of skin tone, but he wasn't much lighter.

The *Sovereign Collective Directorate of A'Zedi* tended to be darker than the *United Technocracy*, as *Wronlori* was officially known. Or *The Holy Imperium of Copez*.

Jocelyn Konicek looked more like a *Wronlori* citizen, but humanity had all hues.

"Glad to know I won't cause you problems," she noted, also rising.

He grinned, but let that one go. They had a mission to complete first.

Then, maybe, some personal time.

If he ever went off duty.

12

Padraig had his A-team on duty today. Watch schedules rotated around to have everyone awake and sharp now, when he needed them.

Two prior stops had yielded nothing. No new buoys, no updates. Nothing, save Jocelyn Konicek walking around in an outfit that more people than him found distracting, though she remained perfectly professional at all times.

He'd made it a point not to be alone with the woman.

"Radio, how does our horizon look?" he called.

Nyssa, Zarah, Maddox. Chance and Magorian aft. Everyone sharp.

"I'm picking up a set of navigational markers, sir," Nyssa replied. "Five of them, each on a different frequency, broadcasting a synchronized time signal."

Padraig nodded. Find any three of them and you could plot your position in this system probably to the meter, given the light-speed lag.

"Anything else?" he continued.

"Inner part of the system is a mess, sir," she said. "Astronautical charts suggest that something happened, early in the star's collapse, to shatter all the smaller planets close in. Lots of rubble out to about two standard units, then a few giants sweeping their orbits clear while also collecting more rubble in the various LaGrange Points. Mostly leading and trailing."

"Understood," Padraig nodded. "Helm, let's sit still here for a bit and quietly watch. Radio, turn on everything passive and listen. Guns, if somebody comes our way, we may be launching and firing everything, then either chasing or running. Keep your crews handy, but start sending them on breaks now."

A trio of assents, and Padraig leaned back to watch.

They'd snuck into the edge of this system slowly. Carefully. Staying well out in the darkness and approaching from a vector similar to what *Northwind* had done, hoping to spot some evidence that would let them know what had happened.

"Update," Nyssa said, her voice calm. "I'm detecting a signal deep in. Loud, like someone is broadcasting a navigational beacon. Roughly about where I would expect a second planet, based on rings of rubble. Really messy down there."

"Station or ship, Radio?" he asked.

"Hard to tell, sir," Nyssa replied. "Lots of highly metallic asteroids floating around, so scans are a mess. Definitely *Wronlori*. Possibly civilian."

"Show me," Padraig ordered.

He looked at his own screen and caught the transmission. Ongoing. On a single channel. They wanted the system to know where they were.

"Sir?" Maddox spoke up from his Gunner station.

Padraig nodded to the man.

"It might be one of these," the man said, sending over a schematic of a factory ship to Padraig's screen. "Big hauler that *Wronlori* frequently uses in situations like this. Move in and start mining various metals, with a small refinery built in that they can use to process the metals on site. Usually as part of setting up some sort of permanent installation, when you don't want to haul a lot of equipment out and aren't in any hurry."

Padraig nodded, seeing the details.

"Let's assume that for now," he told his officers. "That presumes a lot of wildcatters and scouts out looking for interesting things, so stay alert for small ships coming and going. Radio, keep one of your Aetherial scanners pointed inward at all times, so we're tracking if anyone starts coming this way on Ghostdrives."

He paused and considered his options. They were about twenty standard units out right now. Roughly seven light-hours from the star. Dark against a dark background, but he could see the amount of rubble between here and there, and it was almost a fog of small moons and crap floating around.

Useful, because it would hide them. Painful, because they had to find a needle in an enormous haystack, where *Northwind* would be hiding from them as much as they were everyone else.

Plus, he had no way of knowing how closely anyone down there would be watching their own scanners. *The United Technocracy* tended to automate things to a much higher standard that *A'Zedi* felt comfortable with, allowing them to build ships with smaller crews.

The risk was, like with *Northwind*, when something broke and you might not have enough bodies to repair it.

In a situation like this, how many false positives would such a system throw up if you automated things? Padraig was willing to bet a whole bunch.

If he were in charge as a civilian, Padraig could see setting a pretty high threshold and letting the system scan until something important happened.

Had they seen *Northwind*?

"Nevin," Padraig said, turning to his Gunner. "What does a factory like that tell us?"

Maddox paused, pursing his lips.

"Most likely a civilian vessel, sir," he hedged carefully. "Probably as focused as possible on mining, refining, and building. Not sure where they are in the process, but that part tends to be pretty standard. Slow build out that ends with the core of a pretty useful station. Kinda like we saw at Varfelis, but focused on metals instead of gases. Once you have enough, you can start putting out sheets of steel alloys that lets you build more components quickly. If it is automated enough, they might have the dead minimum crew aboard necessary to keep things running, with all the bodies in the factory parts."

"You research that, Guns," Padraig ordered. "Work with Taggart to refine everything we can see from here, listening to radio traffic as well to determine their alert level."

"Sir, I'm not sure I'd use that term," Nyssa spoke up. "Chatter is pretty relaxed and mostly involves dirty jokes interspersed with navigational updates and complaints about claims. I agree with Gunner Nevin that it feels civilian."

"Look for police patrols, then," Padraig ordered. "We're here to scout for rescue, but I'm not above a raid, if the opportunity presents itself as part of everything else. If we could disable the factory, the smaller ships ought to be able to remove the crews to whatever system is closest without a lot of lives lost. Also, see if you can locate *Northwind* close in, like it got disabled and they captured it. What am I missing?"

"Passive defenses," Chance spoke up from her emergency bridge aft. "If something happened to *Northwind* too quickly to call for help, they might have run into something unexpected."

"Would the locals have missed that, though?" Nevin asked.

"Civilians, so they might have," Padraig replied. "Look for mines or captor systems. If one of those went off and *Northwind* took the brunt of it, the locals might have missed that. Or the ship was already captured and removed and we're possibly here to avenge them. I need options people, before we do anything. Chance, you go off duty now and prepare to spell me in a few hours. Everyone else, put in at least one hour now, then start rotations of watch, but nobody go far."

Nods. Heads down and working. Quiet chatter building up as people started assessing things.

He had a mystery on his hands, and the need to solve it quickly.

13

Nyssa studied the system as it was displayed on her screen.

Mess. Millions of small rocks just big enough to show up on optical scans, reflecting light and solar wind in all directions. Hundreds of emitters broadcasting signals, mostly buoys of some sort, though a bunch were small ships flitting around or anchored to some asteroid they were either mining or pushing.

Maddox had sent her a link to study. A civilian mining and processing ship, giving her things to compare to what she could see. Lots of iron and carbon around her. Water in the form of larger rocks and comets floating around.

Everything you needed to survive and build a small, thriving culture, similar to what they'd seen at Varfelis Station. And yet another possible forward base from which *Wronlori* could launch raids on some future date, once enough of an infrastructure got quietly built up here.

Communications showed a half dozen or so small police vessels. Crews under a dozen. Mostly configured for search and rescue from the chatter on open frequencies. Not a particularly heavy hand to their operations.

"Boss, I got something strange," Bex spoke up on her earpiece. "Screen eleven."

Nyssa toggled through and studied the image. *Marrakesh* was too far away to resolve it easily, but Nyssa had access to things Bex didn't, so she fed the image in and let some of those tools wash it and compare.

Took about two seconds to get a match. Nyssa's breath caught.

"Radio?" Captain Boru asked sharply from his station.

"Sending you an image, sir," she said automatically. "Bex, find me the rest of them."

"Rest of them?" the woman asked.

"There will be an entire field like it," Nyssa replied. "Possibly arrayed in an overlapping pattern of coverage."

"Roger that."

Nyssa turned to the captain.

"Those are some extremely serious mines, Radio," he observed neutrally.

"Agreed, sir," she said. "Can I show you something on my screen?"

He rose and moved to stand just over her left shoulder. It was a comforting presence, having him right there. Like he could carry the entire ship on his shoulders.

She'd seen him do it.

"My notes show this as a captor mine, sir," she said, bringing up one of those files that he was about the only other person on the ship qualified to read. "Super-heavy particle beam. One shot. Medium range. Dark both physically as well as electronically. Bex saw it because she was looking sideways and caught it transiting something bright with a shadow."

"And you expect a field of them?" he asked.

"Aye, sir," Nyssa nodded. "The notes suggest that you lay them on approach lines and let someone get too close. I would presume all the local ships have been warned to remain a specific distance away from the area for safety. We're outside what I would expect to be their engagement zone, but we weren't trying to get any closer to the core of the system at the moment."

She turned and watched him stare at something ten thousand light-years away for a long moment.

"Scenario, Radio," he said simply. "*Northwind* did get closer. Or tried to. They encountered one of these and suffered sudden, catastrophic damage. If they were closing, we presume either they got captured, or drifted in too close to everyone else and got destroyed by several more of these mines engaging."

"Also, they might have been hit while withdrawing, sir," Nyssa added. "I've tasked Bex Magorian with finding a gap in the field. Such a thing, if it exists, might narrow down the window where we should look for wreckage or a signal."

"Excellent work, Taggart," he smiled at her. "Right at the moment, you and your team are the most important parts of this mission, so you tell the rest of us what you need. Or issue orders on the fly and presume I'll back you up until I intervene. Am I clear?"

She gasped again, grasping the enormity of what he'd offered.

A captain was always in command. If anything went wrong, they took the blame, even if they'd been asleep at the moment when catastrophe struck. Failure to properly train and supervise their officers and crew was enough to remove someone from command.

And he was handing his entire career into her hands.

Nyssa gulped and nodded.

"Aye, sir," she whispered more than spoke.

"Good," he nodded back. "And keep up the good work."

Nyssa nodded again and went back to her screens.

14

Kaitlin was in the forward section of the repair pod, in a small officer's lounge separate from the vast enlisted crew's quarters that spanned several decks below her. Mostly, she was chatting with Thalia and Jocelyn. Walker was nice enough, but tended to be more formal, even when it wasn't necessary.

It was just the girls at the moment.

She'd considered teasing Padraig about the way he'd been acting around Jocelyn, but decided that she should let that one go, though she had quietly mentioned to the woman that he wasn't very heterosexual, most of the time.

Most of the time. Kaitlin had found Jocelyn to be extremely interesting simply to talk to, with a vast range of experiences and interests. That made the long missions better, when Kaitlin's main job was to keep the newcomers from making cultural mistakes in strange territory.

Thalia checked the time and rose.

"I need to update Walker and see if he's had any surprises," Thalia announced as she made her way to the hatch, mug of tea in one hand. "Don't start any revolutions until I get back."

"Would I do that?" Jocelyn asked in a sassy tone.

"Yes," Thalia laughed and exited.

Kaitlin watched her remaining compatriot chuckle.

"You've got to be crazy to do EVA repair for a living," Jocelyn noted with a grin. "Riskiest single job in the fleet."

"Rush junkie?" Kaitlin asked.

"Absolutely," Jocelyn agreed. "Nothing like that moment of pure power, hanging out there by yourself, moving huge slabs of alloy around, then tack welding them in place for the robots to come in later and finish. Any mistake and you risk getting utterly squished before anybody can do anything to stop that much mass moving."

"Interesting," Kaitlin replied. "I like being inside where it's warm and pleasant. And the hot chocolate is immediately at hand."

Jocelyn laughed out loud, a woman thoroughly enjoying life.

"So are you permanently on the repair side of things?" Kaitlin asked as things settled.

"Yeah," Jocelyn nodded. "At some point, I'll get promoted to Commander like Thalia and have to work inside the station, being the conductor instead of first violin. Until then, I'm spending as much time as possible out in the cold."

"And do you get these sorts of missions regularly?" Kaitlin pressed.

Jocelyn shrugged.

"Being a Forward Repair Depot, we get sent out when someone breaks down too far from home, and on short notice," Jocelyn replied. "Repair frigates are usually stationed forward at various bases, where they can respond to fleet movements or such. *Northwind* isn't the first ship on the wrong side of a line we've gone after. This life is far more interesting than being in a shipyard somewhere."

Kaitlin nodded. Rush junkie seemed to describe a great many of those folks, with Walker Nylund and Commander Leath being perhaps old enough to have grown out of it.

Or to hide it better. There was always that.

She started to say something when a comm chirped. Kaitlin reached out to answer.

"Forward pod. Lynch," she said simply.

"Ma'am, could you ask one of the senior folks aft if they have some time to consult?" Nyssa Taggart asked hesitantly. "I'm pursuing a line of logic and have run into the ends of what I can safely guess. Need an expert."

Kaitlin glanced over and noted that her favorite rush junkie was all eyes and ears, like an excited puppy. She suppressed a laugh.

"I have Knight Konicek in the forward lounge and she seems available," Kaitlin replied. "Should we come forward?"

"If you could," Taggart said. "Captain put me in charge of the operation for now, so I don't want to be far away."

Kaitlin's breath caught at the audacity of such a thing, but she also understood Padraig Boru. And had a pretty good idea how smart Nyssa Taggart really was.

She'd have her own spy ship, one of these days, if she decided she wanted one. Perhaps something like *Northwind*. Everything Padraig had done lately had seen this young woman trained as far as she could go.

And that was a distant horizon.

"We'll be up in a few," Kaitlin said. "Forward conference room or Captain's office?"

"Let's take his office," Taggart replied. "I'll make sure he joins us."

Kaitlin rose and they set off.

Sounded like things were about to get interesting.

More interesting.

Dangerous, even.

15

Padraig had been aft, doing paperwork, when Taggart had summoned him back to his day office.

Well, he had put her in charge.

Kaitlin and Knight Konicek joined them a few moments later.

"I've got Commander Messier and Bex aft, supervising," Nyssa announced as they settled.

His office was large enough for three chairs, though Padraig found himself almost shoulder to shoulder with Konicek. She was still in the skin-tight uniform that left very little to the imagination. All it really hid were tattoos.

He hadn't inquired, unwilling to step into a situation where she offered to show him any she might have. Konicek wasn't in his line of command, but he was still captain of this vessel. And she was an outsider.

She was wearing some faint musk today that smelled of pine trees after a spring rain.

"There is a thing I'm calling a minefield," Taggart began, bringing up a three-dimensional projection with the star at the center.

Padraig watched a band of green appear on the solar ecliptic, a belt around the system about five standard units out. It didn't cover everything, but it did a pretty good job of blocking in those blank areas that wouldn't normally have any ships in them because the planets that far out had swept things reasonably clean, keeping most of the junk closer in.

Inside the wall, as it were, where the little ships were safe to fly and sharks couldn't get at them easily.

"Minefield?" Konicek perked right up. "What kind?"

Nyssa did something on her tablet and the projection slid to one side, replaced by a schematic of a *Wronlori* captor mine. A really mean one, at that.

"Oh, those," Konicek grimaced. "Nasty lot."

"Agreed," Taggart said. "One of my assistants found the first one. From there, we located the entire belt. Or, at least, those portions of it around here where it matters. The array runs in spots around a good chunk of the solar system, on most of the approaches. There are blind spots that are safe. Mostly polar approaches. We're far enough outside that we didn't encounter anything, plus we're running as silent as we can."

"Gotcha," Konicek nodded. "What expertise can I help with?"

Padraig felt the woman lean forward from the heat on his arm as she got closer. Taggart swapped images again, and set an animation in place.

Two new dots appeared in the minefield, then disappeared a moment later.

"Looking at the map as it exists, we predicted two more mines that we were unable to locate," Nyssa said. "Here and here. According to my notes and our Gunner's, these captor mines are really a big nuclear bomb that detonates, lasing a massive particle cannon downrange in the brief instant before it comes apart."

"Wouldn't the locals have noticed something like that?" Kaitlin asked sharply.

"According to Maddox, they are extremely efficient," Taggart shook her head. "It would look like a quasar if it was pointed right at you. Otherwise, it might be invisible. Locals are civilians, and don't seem to be operating at military efficiency."

"Interesting." Kaitlin leaned back.

Konicek leaned in even closer to the image, brushing against Padraig's arm. He held perfectly still.

Taggart studied the woman.

"What happens if two of them went off in close order, firing on a single target?" Nyssa asked.

"Depending on range, it might open a Patrol Cruiser up like a fish on a filleting board," Konicek replied. "I'd presume *Northwind* was running quiet and not evading much, so a beam slamming into their armor might be the first warning that they'd been seen. Have you tracked wreckage?"

"No, but we only just located these two mines," Nyssa replied. "I guessed something along those lines, but this is where I'm outside my normal zone and needed help."

"If they were headed inward, then they were likely seen, because the beam would be pointed at someone," Konicek noted. "You'd get some reaction. I'd guess they were headed into the darkness, based on the gossip that nobody around here seems all that keyed up."

"Agreed," Nyssa said. "One would expect something, if an enemy ship were captured or destroyed around here less than a month ago. Even jokes on open frequencies. There have been none."

She turned to Padraig and he could see the nervousness in her eyes that never made it to her voice.

"Recommend that we withdraw slightly, sir," she began. "Then plot a lateral course on rotary thrusters only that moves us into an area where we can run better passive scans to locate anomalies."

Padraig liked the way she phrased that. Nothing certain. Find something that doesn't fit the pattern, then estimate what it means.

About like hunting a *Wronlori* Leviathan in a nebula and trying to kill it.

Math, patience, and aggression. The mark of a good officer.

He had one here. Three good ones. A whole ship of them, if he could be a bit arrogant about it. Best ship in the damned fleet, in his opinion. And Fleet seemed to agree. He didn't care who complained about his repeating himself.

"You have the bridge, Radio," he said simply. "Plot and execute with Halloran and her people. Keep Nevin in the loop, then make sure that Konicek's people are ready for whatever you need."

He felt Konicek's mild jolt of surprise only because they were physically in contact, so Padraig turned his head far enough to smile at her.

Not far enough for a kiss, but that wouldn't have required much motion from either of them.

"Anything else?" he asked the three of them.

"Nothing here, sir," Nyssa said. "I'm playing a hunch."

"It's a solid one," he assured her.

He rose, but so did Kaitlin and Konicek, and they were between him and the hatch. He was close enough to the woman to dance, but there was a bulkhead immediately behind him.

"Do you have a few moments, Captain?" Konicek asked.

"I do," he replied neutrally.

"Pardon me," Nyssa said, sliding by everyone and exiting to the bridge.

"Jocelyn, I'll see you aft in a bit," Kaitlin announced as she moved in Taggart's wake.

Padraig moved around to his side of the desk and sat. It put the thing between them physically as well as emotionally.

"What can I do for you, Knight?" he asked as the hatch closed.

Konicek studied him for a moment, then grinned for the blink of an eye and sat.

Padraig had a moment of terror at whatever it was that crossed her mind, but he had the desk.

Hopefully, it would protect him.

16

———

Jocelyn studied Captain Boru.

Tall. Darker skinned than her, with straight black hair. Skinny. Handsome, in a rugged way, like a wine that would get better with age.

And young to be a captain. She'd looked him up and he'd been promoted from Knight to Commander to Captain in two months, mostly to put him in command of the refurbishment of this tug.

And he must have impressed someone important to be given command of a blank slate operation like this one.

"What can I do for you, Knight?" he asked as the hatch behind her closed.

Jocelyn kept her commentary to herself and settled.

They were alone, Captain and Knight in his office.

"I appreciate that Squire Taggart is sharp," Jocelyn began delicately. "She really doesn't understand what those mines might have done, if they hit *Northwind*, does she?"

"You might be surprised, Konicek," he replied. "She helped me hunt down and nearly kill a *Wronlori* Leviathan in single combat."

"*Sundering Wrath*," Jocelyn nodded.

She'd looked him and this ship up when the orders came through, wondering if he was the luckiest man alive, the smartest, or the most stubborn.

Maybe all three, after enough time aboard his ship.

Impressive as hell, however you wanted to measure it.

"So I suspect that she understands that *Northwind* might have been terminally damaged," he continued. "However, until we confirm no survivors, she'll operate as if there are people who have no engines and no comm systems, floating helplessly out there in the dark, hoping that something good happens. That's us."

"If they got hit this close in, we won't be able to fully deploy the pod's systems, captain," Jocelyn reminded him.

"Understood," he nodded, compact in his emotions like he was compact in his movements.

Precise in ways that Jocelyn found rare among senior officers. At least the ones who weren't complete assholes.

And Padraig Boru was anything but.

"So what do you expect?" she asked bluntly, mostly to see where he'd go with a blank question.

"My hope is that we find them," he said simply. "Vessel injured too badly to repair or escape themselves, but counting down until they needed to call the locals to rescue them, at which point they go about destroying all the intelligence systems aboard and hope nobody notices. If we can slip in, I'll put all of your people aboard to see if we can salvage things. Failing that, if we can somehow hook up to *Northwind* and tractor them deeper into space without being seen, then you can repair them. Worse come to worst, we rescue the crew, blow the ship in place, and go home."

"Would you attack the system?" she asked, surprised at his own blunt answer.

"Maybe," he shrugged. "Taggart and her people need time to determine if there are sufficient defenses around here to thwart us. We may want to leave them alone so that a raiding squadron can return at a later date and do the job thoroughly. My assignment is to find and rescue *Northwind*'s crew. Everything else is secondary and will be determined by circumstances when we get there. Does that help?"

"It does," Jocelyn nodded, all the more impressed by his calm demeanor as he walked through the options.

No bluster. No anger.

Pure calm professionalism. Not quite the exact opposite of her, but really close across the way.

And she'd seen the way he watched her, though he'd always retained that sharp professionalism that she found even more intriguing. Some officers would have gotten more friendly. Others more aloof.

He walked right down a most interesting path.

Jocelyn nodded to herself and rose.

"Is that all you needed today?" Captain Boru asked as she did.

"Today," she agreed, noting the way his eyes took all of her in.

She'd never been the prettiest. The tallest. The whateverist.

Jocelyn Konicek had, however, worked twice as hard as everyone else. And might have frequently been among the smartest in the room.

Not on this ship, though. Boru had some amazing people around him. And she was beginning to understand why.

And maybe she'd have to take the lead when they were done and headed home from a successful mission.

Like him, job first, but then there'd be time for other things later.

Right now, she needed to brief Walker and Thalia.

And get everyone ready for something even more crazy than usual.

17

Zarah Halloran had the bridge at the moment. At her station instead of the captain's, but she could have sat there.

Growing into her job, but Zarah put that down to her time on *Marrakesh*. Captain Boru was one of those officers who believed that all of his officers and crew should be as trained and ready to take over as possible, at any minute.

Plus, they'd had adventures well beyond what a simple Tactical Transport should normally have undertaken. It was good.

Middle of ship's night. Everyone was pulling longer hours than normal, but she'd volunteered to let Commander Messier get some extra sleep by standing an extra watch. Glen Tameron had Radio watch at the moment, with Nyssa and Bex Magorian hopefully asleep.

"Sir?" Glen perked up, typing suddenly across his entire screen. "I've got something."

"My screen number one," she ordered, looking closer as he echoed things. "How the hell did you even see that, Tameron?"

"Squire Taggart told us to look for black on black, sir," he grinned. "Something about ships like *Northwind* being built to hide from sensor probes and painted with the least reflective stuff available. Anything to gain another basis point of hiding."

Zarah nodded. Nyssa had mentioned that it would be hard to see, if they found the ship.

"Hit them with a quiet IR scan, Tameron," she ordered, not quite ready to rouse the captain from sleep, but her mind had marked that button on the keyboard. "I want to know if that thing is above expected ambient for solar wind, this far out."

"Aye, sir. Stand by."

Zarah waited on pins and needles. They weren't that far away from the anomaly, but not all that close either. Well under a light-minute, and could close the distance relatively quickly if necessary.

However, that might also be a *Wronlori* ship, hiding in the darkness for pirates or *A'Zedi* vessels like hers to wander too close. Like, say, someone had recently been captured spying in this system and the locals wanted to lay a trap for anyone coming to save them.

In which case, they might open fire without any warning. Missiles could already be in flight, inbound at high speed, before someone detected them over there.

Zarah weighed everything and opened the rocker switch at the top of her station's keyboard. Then she slammed a palm down on the alert button.

Better safe than sorry.

"All hands to alert stations," she announced over the intercom.

Zarah left it at that, because really she was getting folks where they needed to be now. Captain Boru regularly ran such exercises, mostly to keep people sharp.

She wanted the sharp end of the stick pointed downrange if she needed it.

Maddox Nevin appeared first, wearing sleeping pants and an undershirt, socks in one hand that he set on his station as he bumped Specialist Doherty from Gunner. Kellen moved to a secondary station around the outside and brought it live, rather than move elsewhere.

Nyssa and Captain Boru were hip-to-hip through the hatch. Both came to rest nearby, but didn't immediately take over.

"Status?" the captain asked.

"Anomaly located, sir," Tameron explained. "Main screen. Heat signature shows power being dumped outside the vessel. Hard to identify them at this range."

Zarah nodded. Best that he bring them up to speed. She was watching a perimeter sweep while Maddox and his gun crews limbered up.

"Have they made any indications they've seen us?" Boru asked.

"Negative, sir," Zarah interjected. "Taking the safe path there before approaching an unknown and possibly hostile vessel in deep space."

"And the correct choice, Squire," he nodded. "I am taking command."

"Transferring command, sir," Zarah replied, feeling the weight slide off her shoulders like a wet cloak.

She'd been at her station already, so Zarah didn't have to move.

"Glen, I'll take over, but don't go far," Nyssa said.

They swapped and he moved to a station next to Kellen Doherty on the outer rim of things, bringing it live.

"All stations report green for combat operations," Zarah announced, tracking that portion of things, even as Captain Boru had assumed command.

"Plot me a course that moves us closer, Halloran," he said. "But keep the rotary thrusters angled away from the center of the system so nobody can happen to see our flare."

Zarah frowned at that, then understood. *Marrakesh* was running silent and dark, but the engines had to push, and that created a light. Maybe it pointed at someone and caused them to wake up. To ask questions. To report their own anomaly to someone else, triggering a patrol ship of some sort to come looking.

Or send an Aetherial signal home, screaming for the *Wronlori* fleet to send a warship to save them. Exactly what *Marrakesh* didn't want today.

Zarah keyed the comm aft.

"Engineering. Carpenter Garber."

Senior enlisted crew back there. Ahearn might be slow to react. Or busy fixing something.

"Carpenter, I need to bring up thrust," Zarah announced. "And we'll be imparting a bit of a corkscrew spin to the vessel at the moment, in order to get the vector I need. Stand by to bring all your generators and engines fully online for this, just in case."

"Gimme thirty seconds," he countered. "Warming everything now saves us a lot of wear and tear later, unless you need it."

"Thirty seconds is fine, Garber," she told him. "Send a signal forward when your board is fully green."

"Aye, sir."

She cut the line and studied her plot. Anything would flash a light in towards the center of the system, but if she wobbled in the process, the light wouldn't last long on any line. Hopefully, nobody would notice it. Or they'd put it down to solar wind fluorescing off of something.

Anything but an intruder.

"Captain, I'm ready here," she announced after a minute.

"As you bear, Squire," he replied.

Zarah smiled and nodded.

She'd been trained to expect a commanding officer who wanted an excessive amount of detail before anything was done. The folks at the Academy pounded that into the students. Captain Boru was something of a unicorn, trusting that he didn't have to look over her shoulder at every moment and second guess each and every little thing she did.

The mark of a bad officer, he'd said more than once.

Zarah typed in the command and heard the camber of the ship change as it slowly accelerated onto a new, curving path that would hopefully bring them close enough to *Northwind* to identify it.

Assuming anyone had survived.

18

Nyssa studied the sensor readings. Everything was still passive, but Glen had turned up the infrared sensitivity enough to confirm that there was heat on over there.

Neither ship was emitting anything detectable at any range, not counting the rotary thrusters, so it was hard to make anything out.

"Radio," Captain called. "Status?"

"Quiet, sir," she replied. "A hole in space, just like us."

She'd even made sure that none of the external navigational lights could be turned on by personally overriding their controls. *Marrakesh* was a gray whale sailing blithely along, seeking a black one in the middle distance.

"Taggart, I think we're lateral enough," Zarah said quietly. "You might be able to send a scan without it being seen."

Nyssa studied the plot. Took a moment, then she saw it. Zarah hadn't gone directly towards the anomaly, but had maneuvered the ship sideways, until they were nearly the same distance out from the sun.

Any scan she sent now wouldn't be pointed at another ship closer in, though some might be able to detect anything that bounced back.

Nyssa dialed down the emitter to the lowest power that would reflect off the hull over there and return. Then brought it up a bit when she remembered that *Northwind*—if that's what this was—wouldn't have as great a signal return.

Nothing grand. Simply pointing a series of lasers over there and trying to get a rough estimate of the shape.

Time passed. The signals only moved at light-speed. Then returned and had to be processed.

Shape was immediately obvious. Longer than it was tall. Possibly tumbling on the long axis, but slowly.

Like a derelict.

Generally the smooth curves of a warship, where designers still streamlined things, in spite of having ships that never entered an atmosphere to need it.

Aesthetics.

"Captain, I have a reasonable match to an *A'Zedi* cruiser hull," Nyssa said aloud, forcing her voice up from a whisper so that everyone would hear. "No signal, but I haven't tried to contact them, either."

"Guns, bring all your teams to full combat readiness," Captain Boru said distinctly. "If this is a trap, I want a set of Sixes through him like nails."

"Understood, sir," Maddox replied. "Tubes loaded. Particle cannons and railgun pulsars are live."

"Radio, how close do you need to be to scan them effectively?" the captain asked.

"About a third closer, sir," Nyssa guessed, based on the signal returns so far.

"Helm, bring us around and start inward," he continued. "Engineering, Ghostdrives are live?"

"At a moment's notice, sir," Garber answered from aft.

Everything was poised.

If it was a trap, they'd done everything they could to mitigate the danger.

Now *Marrakesh* had to sail in and risk everything.

Nyssa brought up as many things as she could point at the other vessel and tried to paint them with lasers to study the shape.

At the same time, she sent a coded pulse, also via tight-beam laser, hoping that someone was awake and paying attention.

Or at least alive to hear her.

The anomaly was still a hole in space on most of her screens.

Slowly, the signals resolved. The shape matched up, with jagged tears down one flank and across the aft. One hole in the outer hull looked like a harpoon had gotten home, punching a gaping wound all the way through the vessel side to side and possibly through three decks oblong.

On her screen, a blue light flashed.

It took her a moment to understand that someone on the wreckage had turned on a marker.

Then it blinked. Rapidly. Not randomly, either.

"Sir, I have a signal from the derelict," Nyssa called. "Binary code. Stand by while they transmit."

She was holding her breath. Around her, everyone else had that same poise as they worked.

Binary. On. Off. Long. Short. Slow and tedious way to send information, but hopefully someone had detected her laser, even if they didn't have the equipment to reply adequately.

"I've identified us as *Marrakesh*, sir," Nyssa continued, a running commentary for everyone else. "Return message indicates *Northwind*. Damage extensive. Crew trapped but alive. Requesting rescue."

"Let them know that we're here," Captain Boru said. "Get as much information as you can from the signal, and tell them that we'll dock as soon as possible."

"Aye, sir," she replied.

Nyssa concentrated on packing as much information as she could into the fewest words possible.

Repair tug Marrakesh. *Closing quickly. Radio silent. Stand by for rescue.*

And transmit.

Over her metaphorical shoulder, she kept a watch on the inner portions of the solar system. Then typed a number.

"Secondary bridge. Magorian."

"Bex, you take over all sensors pointed at anything inside the minefield," Nyssa ordered. "Keep them from sneaking up on us. If you detect something, route it to Armiger Nevin for his gun teams to engage. Do not keep me in that loop, as I'll be focused on *Northwind*."

"Roger that," Bex replied. "Taking over rear watch."

Nyssa nodded and cut the line, tuning all of that out of her mind.

Now was the riskiest portion of the mission, because they had to get close enough to talk directly, while making sure that nobody else saw anything on any sensor that caused them to come investigate.

Or attack.

"Glen, watch my close perimeter for anyone lying in wait," Nyssa turned to the man. "Same orders as Bex. Route them to Nevin immediately for combat. Assume a trap if anything unmasks."

"Aye, sir," Glen nodded.

Nyssa drew a breath. She turned to Captain Boru.

"What am I missing, sir?"

He smiled warmly.

"Nothing, at present," he nodded. "We're on approach. We're quiet. We're about to fulfill at least part of our mission."

"Security," Nyssa barked.

He studied her without speaking, one eyebrow raised.

"They might have captured the ship, and put a team of invaders aboard to storm *Marrakesh* when we docked," Nyssa said.

"I've already let Farrell know," he replied. "She's got her people ready to escort Konicek's folks when I clear them to board."

Nyssa blew out heavily and nodded.

She returned to her screens and tried to estimate how badly *Northwind* had been hurt.

It looked ugly from the outside.

19

―――――

Padraig studied the scans as Nyssa's computers assembled tidbits and made estimations. Her software was light-years better than anything he'd had expected aboard a line warship, so her capabilities were equally impressive.

It added up to a mess.

He dialed a number.

"Forward pod. Lynch."

"Kaitlin, do you have everyone handy?" he asked.

"They are, Padraig," she said. "Go ahead."

"Folks, I'm sending some scanner logs," Padraig said, transmitting things. "Security will board the ship first, but Knight Konicek will need to be right behind them so she can give me a first level approximation as quickly as possible. I dare not deploy the full depot this close in, so we need to know if *Northwind* can be towed, repaired, or if it needs to be blown in place. Time is critical at present, because we will be broadcasting more signals as we work, and someone might notice. Assuming that this isn't one of several traps. Knight Konicek, you will be armed when boarding *Northwind*, as will the rest of your crew."

He heard the gasps and mutters over the intercom, and ignored them.

This was a combat situation until he was satisfied that it wasn't.

And only then.

Captain of this vessel. Not even Walker Nylund could pull rank on that. Other things, sure, but those occurred after the initial emergency was over.

"Captain, this is Nylund."

"Go ahead," Padraig replied.

"Suggest you deploy Jocelyn and a three-person team initially," Nylund said. "If you feed us real-time data here, Thalia and I can start assessing repair priorities from the outside. Heat suggests that at least some generators are working over there, but that puncture aft appears to have gone directly through engineering itself. We'll need to know if they have Ghostdrives or rotary thrusters available, most likely first."

"Understood," Padraig replied. "If you can get your team aft to the primary cargo airlocks, I have Lead Security Expert Cameron Farrell assembling her team there now. Security Expert Trinh Lành Hoàng will be holding the airlock while we have teams off-vessel."

"Excellent, Captain," Nylund said. "Thank you and we will get you the information you need as quickly as humanly possible."

Padraig nodded to himself and cut the line.

Northwind had been slashed once and punched about as hard as possible. They were probably fortunate that it had been a heavy particle cannon beam instead of a missile fragment, because the latter would have likely taken out most of the rear third of the ship, instead of just punching starlight through.

More survivors, now that *Marrakesh* was handy to help.

There would still be a lot of dead from something like this. Unfortunate, but war was like that, and *Wronlori* didn't seem to ever prefer peace. Hell, their surprise attack at *Eworn* nearly four years ago had merely started the most recent war.

Or most recent flaring up.

Wronlori never seemed to choose peace.

Even this system looked like a great place from which to eventually stage raids on *A'Zedi* systems.

Padraig might still have to do something about that. But not today.

Today, he had a rescue to organize.

20

Cameron Farrell was the only full-time combat trooper on the ship. Everyone else had at least one other job, from damage control to wardroom. Even Trinh worked part time with the Quartermaster, handling supplies.

Cam got to train a lot. There were a vast range of things to know and practice. And a variety of manuals to study and master, in order to train her people in things that they might encounter exactly once in their entire career.

Like boarding a potentially captured vessel filled with enemy agents in *A'Zedi* uniforms.

Fortunately, she had Squire Taggart on her side. Bad guys were doomed.

She checked her suit one last time, then turned to Specialist Lorenzen. Studied the boy. BIG. Not the sharpest spoon in the drawer, but probably the toughest. Cam generally used him as a training dummy on account of a high pain threshold that let her hit him without doing much damage. When she might break someone smaller. Holding a tablet computer delicately in one hand.

"You type and confirm," Cam ordered. "Understood?"

"Yes, ma'am," he nodded.

She looked him in the mouth, even as tall as she was. And was maybe two-thirds as wide, even with her muscles and mass.

Right now, she needed him pulling up the personnel files that Taggart had loaded onto the tablet in his hands, while Cam held a gun on folks.

Anybody trying to wrestle got Lorenzen to dance with. About as safe as arguing with a bear.

Cam looked around at the others. Her usual boarding team, minus Trinh, who had to hold the fort here against dipshits pulling a bum's rush on the hatch.

"Trinh?" Cam asked on the headset.

"You're locked out," Cam's sidekick chuckled. "Gonna have to ask me real nice if you want back in again later."

"As long as you shoot anyone else first," Cam laughed.

"Oh, don't you worry, buttercup."

Cam had checked out the Light Disruptor Cannon to Trinh earlier. Nobody was going to be a problem with that around.

Cam turned to the officer next. Woman wasn't in charge. Wasn't even in the chain of command. Smart enough to understand that, too, since being a Knight was usually good for being important.

"We'll clear the initial situation," she reminded Konicek. "At that time, you'll be able to communicate with the locals, but only after I'm satisfied that they are who they claim. If shit breaks out, I expect you to engage any unknown hostiles with enough force to repulse them. Don't worry about hunting people down and killing them later. If they turn out to be a problem, that's my job anyway. Questions, sir?"

"None here, Farrell," Konicek nodded. "Captain Boru ordered me to submit to your authority until you were satisfied by the situation."

Cam nodded.

They'd have to physically drag her ass off this ship if they wanted to transfer her elsewhere. Assuming Captain Boru was still in command. If he left, Cam would take just about any transfer, because even Commander Messier wasn't going to be as good, let alone a total stranger.

Cam took one more look around her team. Small because cramped quarters and risk. The rest of them were hiding behind Lorenzen, because he was a brick wall that walked.

She drew her Adjustable Disruptor and went right ahead and dialed it down to the setting where it would knock the average human on his ass and maybe crack a few ribs. Sometimes a polite stun was acceptable. Sometimes you wanted them dead.

Cam figured she should make a statement, if she ended up needing to shoot anyone.

She holstered it, but she could still draw faster than just about anyone.

"Bridge, this is Farrell," she announced to whoever was monitoring things. "We're ready here."

"Stand by," Squire Halloran replied. "Docking in thirty seconds, then we'll lock things and kill their spin with gyros and thrusters here. Everybody grab onto something just in case."

Cam had a hand on a bar placed exactly for that purpose, because sometimes you had to kill gravity when doing things like this.

She counted noses and statuses. Everyone in suits with sufficient armor for EVA, but not the heavy stuff she'd have on for a storming action.

Supposedly, friendlies on the other side of the wall.

Supposedly.

Noises as the two ships came together at an extended docking airlock. Thumps as rings and hooks engaged and pulled the two into a single entity. Local Gravity Field Emitters were up to the task, but there was still a jolt as things settled. Mostly the sort of thing you felt in the inner ear, rather than the ribs.

Silence.

"Security team, we have lock and positive pressure on both sides of the hatch," the call came. "You make the call."

"Security team, in motion," Cam replied.

She nodded to everyone and stepped up. One hand triggered the hatch and it opened.

She'd left her faceshield open for now, but it would slam shut automatically in a variety of situations. Better this way to hear and smell.

Smoke, but the old kind, where it'd mostly been scrubbed out of the air and was in filters that should have been changed at some point. Faint iron smell she knew indicated blood that had splattered with zero gravity, then dried on walls later.

Mark of starship combat, and she'd been in a few of those.

She studied the woman standing on the other side. Gravity was on over there, but felt wonky. Cam assumed generators holding out well past stability.

Commander, by rank. Haggard redhead with lines that someone had etched into her face with a chisel and a maul. Unarmed, which was really what Cam cared about at the moment.

"Lead Security Expert Farrell," Cam introduced herself. "Permission to come aboard?"

"Welcome, Farrell," the woman said in a voice that didn't mask exhaustion. The kind that you couldn't fake. Unless you were that good of an actor. "Commander Artemis Kingston, acting captain of *Northwind*."

Cam winced as she slipped through the hatch like she was clearing a room. All sides and up. Ready to punch first, shoot second, then ask questions of the survivors.

Kingston didn't move, so she didn't draw any attention. The rest of the room was empty of people.

Acting Captain meant that Ethan Harrington was either dead or disabled.

"What's your status, Commander?" Cam asked, feeling Lorenzen loom up behind her and to one side.

His job was to confirm her against Taggart's records and say something if Cam needed to shoot.

Silence was a good sign.

"We took two hits from something that didn't bother finishing us off," Kingston replied. "Bridge and Engineering were instantly destroyed. Secondary bridge missed being hit by about half a meter, or the ship might have been lost almost completely. Crew casualties were about thirty percent killed in the first day. Another twenty percent succumbed to injuries too great to treat. I've got about thirty percent walking wounded and the rest trying to hold on as long as we could. You really are *A'Zedi*?"

"We are," Cam assured the woman. "Didn't think to bring you any Derby Burgers from Horwin before we left, but the wardroom's pretty good at a close imitation. I've got security folks with me to inspect the vessel, plus repair engineers. What do we need to see first?"

She watched the woman relax. Shoulders came down. Creases in her face softened. She breathed once and Cam could almost taste the exhaustion.

"Engineering is open to space, Farrell," Kingston replied. "Bridge is as well, but Secondary is intact. I have most of my people centralized and a bit aft. We're limited in what repairs we can even attempt due to personnel, but there are enough systems aft working that we have life support and some power. Not a lot, but enough to hang on."

"Fleet's here now, Commander," Cam said simply. "We'll take care of you. You lead and let's get folks in motion."

Behind her, Cam counted noses. Her goons first. Konicek and a handful of her folks after that. Trinh would close things up and keep watch, but nobody was boarding *Marrakesh* without passwords at this point. And guns pointed at them.

It was a dangerous life. Shit happened.

At least *Marrakesh* had gotten here in time.

Hopefully.

21

Jocelyn moved quietly in the big security trooper's wake, but Lorenzen had made it clear that he was there to absorb fire that might hurt someone important.

Serious mindset, from a guy holding a tablet and looking up names and faces instead of watching for trouble.

Jocelyn found herself really impressed by Farrell's people. And Boru's, because he had to have made this sort of behavior possible. And expected.

Sharpest crew she could remember working with in a long time.

Around her, *Northwind* was a wreck. Two hits, one a knife wound gouged out of the starboard flank having ripped open the entire bridge in an instant. The other punching engineering through and through. And possibly coming that close to killing the secondary bridge as well.

Kill a starship that way, if you lost power and command all at once, deep in enemy territory.

And nobody, it seemed, had seen the shots. Or heard the mine speak up afterwards.

Made little sense, but everything pointed to this system being a completely civilian operation.

Had the *Wronlori* navy purposefully left the locals in the dark? That actually added up, if this wasn't a military operation yet.

Later, maybe, but even *A'Zedi* would be hard-pressed to cross the line and attack a place like this without a good reason. Even today, they'd sent a Scout Cruiser to investigate first, rather than a battle squadron.

And Jocelyn and her people, to help rescue *Northwind*.

If they could.

Jocelyn followed as the security team went deeper into the ship. Patrol Cruiser. Reconfigured for long-sailing, so running a significantly smaller crew, with more supplies to let them stay at sea for a long time.

Or die slowly in the darkness.

The tour didn't take long. The damaged parts were currently open to space for the most part. The rest were support and hull elements that hadn't taken much damage, though Jocelyn could see places where overloads had short-circuited things by the way certain juncture boxes were blackened all the way around.

Farrell and Kingston stopped at a frame hatch with flashing red lights indicating vacuum beyond.

Engineering.

So far, they'd met about a half-dozen folks. Lorenzen hadn't said anything at any point, so Jocelyn presumed that all were who they appeared to be.

And every single one of them looked like death warmed over, even with that silent spark of hope that had come into their eyes seeing strangers.

What must it be like, trapped and alone, with the options of hoping for rescue, or having to call the enemy and hope that they decided to take you prisoner instead of just standing back and finishing off the ship for good?

"End of the road," Kingston announced sourly.

Jocelyn nodded and turned in place.

"Can we close off this hallway and turn it into a temporary airlock?" she asked the woman.

Kingston blinked several times as her brain caught up. Farrell had moved quietly off to one side, seemingly ceding the situation to the repair team.

Lorenzen seemed satisfied. That seemed sufficient.

Which put Jocelyn on the spot.

Right where she liked to be.

"Probably," Kingston finally said. "You won't want to do it that often, as it won't be very efficient, but it would work for now."

"Easier than backing out and approaching via the holes," Jocelyn explained. "I still plan to do that, but it would be useful to see things from the inside, as it were, first."

"Do you need any of my people, sir?" Farrell asked simply.

Jocelyn turned to Kingston.

"Open to space," Jocelyn said simply. "Any expectation of dead crew members still in place, or would they have been blown entirely clear?"

"They were probably killed instantly by the beam," Kingston grimaced. "I doubt that any were alive five minutes later, anyway. But we've had no communications with anyone from that instant until you pinged us with that laser."

Jocelyn nodded. Turned back to Farrell.

"I'll eventually need as many of the current crew as possible to help point things out to my people," Jocelyn explained. "And any spare hands, since Captain Boru expects us to see what repairs can be undertaken here. Right now, however, maybe we should look at organizing medical evacuations?"

"Doctor Hyden and Counselor Chaudhary are already setting things up aft, sir," Farrell nodded. "Just waiting for the word from us on what to expect."

Jocelyn blinked. She was used to dead ships needing repair, but didn't generally deal with the crews directly. Usually just voices on the comm, because she was outside in her suit, EVA-ing all over the place.

This was more Thalia's job. And maybe hers, one of these days.

"You handle that with Commander Kingston," Jocelyn ordered. She could do that now, as they'd moved to repair and rescue mode. "I'll take Mathias Ryan here with me and we'll step inside. Everyone else with Farrell and report back to Walker. Mathias and I will enter *Marrakesh* via a secondary airlock in a bit."

Farrell looked a bit askance at the situation, but she was Security. And not used to walking around outside on hulls. Not like Jocelyn.

She turned to Mathias. Expert sailor. Built lithe and skinny like a swimmer, which made a certain bit of sense when you had to swim through open space to do things.

"You clear the space and seal up the hallway behind us when they are gone," Jocelyn ordered. "I'll take the forward hatch."

She reached up and triggered her faceplate to seal up for vac operations and checked that everything was solid. She'd basically lived in this mode for more than a week now, so it was all good. Behind her, Ryan got them isolated and Jocelyn went to work on convincing the local systems to airlock for her, drawing all the atmosphere out so she could open this hatch and see what things looked like beyond.

"Captain to Repair Team," Boru's voice intruded as she worked.

Jocelyn smiled and kept typing.

"Konicek."

"Secondary airlock entry later?" he asked carefully, so he'd already gotten everything from Farrell that quickly.

"Pickup by *Flight of Fancy* or *Roadrunner* would be acceptable as well," she replied, naming *Marrakesh*'s two shuttles. "Ryan and I will walk the outer hull as well as Engineering, in order to determine if the effort of repair is worth it."

"Understood, Konicek," Boru said. "ETA?"

"Probably ninety minutes for us, Captain," she replied. "Going to take my time here."

"Roger that," he said simply. "I'll notify flight deck. Captain out."

Jocelyn nodded. Things had kind of inverted now, but that was normal for her. The tug that carried the Forward Repair Depot was the most important thing in the galaxy, right up to the moment when it deployed repair teams.

Then Walker was senior. And Thalia. And even Jocelyn.

Might be all sorts of fun later.

Right now, she finished keying the hatch and watching it slowly open.

22

Jocelyn had been aboard ships gutted like fish. Modern weapons could be dulled by armor, but not defeated.

And this had been a heavy captor mine at short range. One beam, dead centered on Engineering and almost enough to kill the secondary bridge as well.

No sound now but her own breathing. Occasional chatter on the radio, but she and Mathias had moved to channel sixteen to work. Like normal when out in the darkness alone.

He was two steps behind her, holding a short-range rescue harpoon. Compressed air would fire a projectile that cracked open and stuck to something with goop, attached to a line to draw it back to you if someone lost hull contact and didn't have an EVA suit.

Like now.

Simple repair armor in their case, designed to be rugged when dealing with sharp edges, but not fully armored. Electromagnets on her boots turned on to keep her attached. Time to explore.

Open to space. Two holes all the way through, with one about a meter wide over her left shoulder and a gouge through the deck at an oblong angle to her right, where it had kept going out the other side.

Most of the surfaces she could see showed melt damage, but the temperature in here alone would have been lethal, even in most armors. Looking around, no bodies floating in the space. Either instantly destroyed, or sucked out one of the holes when the atmosphere vented.

A quick death, hopefully.

"You wait here," Jocelyn ordered Mathias, waiting for his nod before she proceeded.

The space was a large volume, spanning three decks with catwalks and gantries ranging around generators and engine systems. Dark, with no air to diffuse the few lights.

Jocelyn moved to the main generator bank and studied things with her helmet lights. Four of them across, like small hills. One off, with flashing red lights indicating internal damage. One shut down and possibly off at the time of impact.

Two holding their own against entropy. For now.

She talked to Mathias as she went, but knew that everyone else was monitoring and recording her for later. Easier if it was a flowing conversation, rather than a formal debrief.

"It looks like number three here can be checked and brought back on line pretty quickly," she began. "Four will require a rebuild that might involve dismantling it, so we'll hold that for later. Port fuel line to the rotary thrusters was ruptured, so it probably added a fireball on top of everything else in here before cutouts shut it down. Starboard side looks intact, so we might be able to bring them on line at some point."

"How bad are the holes?" Mathias asked.

"The deck looks like we could weld down a few plates, then caulk it," she replied. "The port side is probably going to require that we build a plug to cover the outside, then maneuver it into place with one or both of the shuttles. More work, but that lets us access storage on that side that's currently cut off by vacuum gaps. I'll get pictures of it when we exit that side."

"Roger that," Mathias replied. "I'm moving lateral to get

some images of gravity and life support controls. Those appear intact from here."

"Agreed," she said, moving deeper. "One shot through. Line cruiser would have probably been in better shape, with double the crew, but I understand that they were lean here and had other troubles. Plus, they have secondary systems forward that were able to hold things together."

"Repair priorities?" he asked, like he usually did.

Thalia and Walker would make those decisions, but she was here, now, and had eyes on. They'd be reviewing her notes, at least until the teams got in and got all this pressurized.

It was like triaging patients. Find the ones needing only a little work, and get them set aside. Identify the ones who couldn't be saved and make them comfortable. Get the ones in the middle and go like hell to save them.

Northwind could be saved. Probably, she amended herself.

If they were in the middle of nowhere, it would take about a week to get everything ready to fly. Deploy the depot like the arms of an octopus around the ship and flood her crews in. Borrow folks from *Marrakesh* and the original crew, then work them like stolen mules.

She didn't have that luxury, parked and drifting in the middle of a *Wronlori* system, trying to be quiet while working. That meant limited EVA, because you needed radios to coordinate things. Bad idea.

Some messages could be done with semaphore, but she'd have to have folks aboard the shuttles she needed, and teach them the language. Or just oust them and fly it herself.

That was always an option, and she was EVA Lead here.

"Power first," she finally answered, circling back to Ryan's question. "Then life support, once we can run all of our heavy tools simultaneously. Plug the holes aft and pressurize. That gets engineers in to inspect and fix rotary thrusters and Ghostdrives. Walker, are you on the line?"

They were inside the ship, and all that metal was a fantastic

Faraday cage. At the same time, you could transmit through your boots and someone else touching hull metal could pick up the signal. Signal relays would connect at the airlocks.

"I'm here, Jocelyn," Walker replied a moment later. "What do you need?"

"When you have a chance, could you ask Captain Boru how long he thinks we'll be able to work?"

"He's standing next to me, Jocelyn, so I'll let him answer."

Jocelyn grinned. Of course he was aft. He had a crew good enough to run things without him breathing down their necks.

"Everything I presume hinges on an unknown clock counting down, Konicek," Boru replied a moment later. "We'll only have minutes at most, if someone goes to Ghost-space headed this direction. If it's one of those police cutters, we can chase them off or destroy them, but then the authorities will call for a fleet to oust us. I have no idea how quickly a Line Cruiser could arrive, and even two of us couldn't defeat something like that, assuming *Northwind* could fight."

"So everything ready to run on a moment's notice?" she asked, intrigued but also angered by his correct logic.

All this effort to save the ship, and they might still have to destroy it at the last minute?

Damn it.

"I would prefer if you included a team confirming that the scuttling charges were intact and ready to activate, as part of your inspection, Knight," Boru added.

Yes, of course. Can't let a ship like this fall into enemy hands, even if the crew escapes safely.

The remainder of the crew.

"Will add it to the checklist, Captain," she replied. "Mathias, I've seen what I need here. Let's work our way out onto the hull and walk the engines. Thalia, you can send folks in to look at other places, but Engineering needs to be the center of our activity for at least a couple of days."

"Understood, Jocelyn," Thalia replied. "I'll start routing

teams in now. Doctor Hyden is handling evacuations for medical needs."

Jocelyn nodded to herself.

So much work to do. But they had the people and tools.

As long as they had the time.

23

———

Padraig headed forward to the corridor where Commander Hyden had put her field hospital. *Marrakesh* was a cruiser hull, with a lot of space, even minus the chunk out of the spine where the double pod got plugged in. The architects had assumed a much larger crew than he had, so Padraig had a massive overflow of unused bunks, because he hadn't let folks spread out any more than they would on any other vessel.

Most of that space had been crammed full of supplies, since nobody knew how long they'd be out, or what shape *Northwind* would be in if they found it. Already, Doc Hyden had folks moving boxes around so that *Northwind*'s crew could be accommodated. As long as nobody had to turn off gravity, they'd be fine.

Or chasing boxes down. Life happened.

Padraig found Elsy supervising her nursing staff and issuing orders to Squire Quinn Nakada, Ship's Nurse.

"Anything else, ma'am?" Nakada asked, smiling.

"No," Elsy grumbled. "Let them sort out who needs to come first. I presume the walking wounded, then we'll get in and move the bedridden."

"On it," Nakada said, then nodded at Padraig. "Sir."

And he was gone.

Padraig slid into the space vacated.

Elsy looked up at him. Short woman. Squat without being overweight. Just solid, like a concrete and steel bollard. Golden-brown skin. Brown eyes that didn't have any mischief today.

"Padraig," she nodded.

"Checking in," he replied. "Seeing if you needed bodies at present, but it looked like you already grabbed them."

"As soon as Taggart's folks found something, I assumed rescue and grabbed the civilians to move things around," she nodded. "My staff have been listening in, and already most of them are aboard *Northwind*. Quinn will start routing them to me next, and I'll use all this as a field hospital."

She gestured down the corridor, where people were coming and going with speed and deliberation. Exactly what you needed in an emergency of unknown proportions.

"You heard Kingston's notes?" he asked.

"I did," she grimaced. "A Patrol Cruiser like that should have somewhere around one hundred and fifty crew. She's currently got twenty-eight fully operational, with another sixty or so injured to some degree that impedes them. Mostly broken limbs and recovery from various concussions when the ship flexed hard under them. I'll be doing a lot of cranial inspections and possibly some drilling to relieve pressure in the short term. We'll likely empty the pharmacology vaults quickly, as well."

Padraig shivered. Meatball surgery, Elsy had called it at one point. You couldn't wait for the drugs to get to work, especially if the patient's system was already shocky, so you bored a hole in their skull and let the pressure out. Then patched them up later and let the medicine bring things back down more deliberately.

When you were certain that they'd survive.

"Are we better off shutting down all gravity on both ships to move people?" Padraig asked.

"It would not hurt in the slightest, but I have no idea where things stand, beyond medical," she shook her head. "Ask Kaitlin."

"I'll make arrangements," Padraig assured her. "You talk to Kaitlin, Chance, or me if you need anything. One of us will be awake."

"Thank you, Padraig," she sighed. "I'll likely need the wardroom sending my coffee regularly to keep me sharp."

"Remember to sleep at some point, Elsy," he reminded her. "We'll spend a few days here just determining what we can do. From there, I'll expect you to brief me on what we'll need to do about crew."

"Based on what Commander Kingston sent, those twenty-eight have been doing everything, while the others watched each other," Elsy said. "They'll collapse at some point, so you might work for now with your crew and the engineers exclusively. I'll send you the others after they all sleep for twelve or twenty hours."

"Sounds good," he agreed. "I'll get out of your hair now."

He nodded and withdrew as Elsy Hyden spun up a whirlwind of activity.

They'd managed the hardest part of the mission, finding *Northwind*.

Now, they had to get everyone home.

24

Nyssa had taken to pulling double watches on the quiet bridge. *Northwind*'s crew didn't need to know what she really did. A few of them would immediately understand, and all could keep their mouths shut or they wouldn't be in that portion of the service, but the fewer people who knew who she was, the fewer risks.

Plus, it let Bex and Glen help repair electronics on the derelict, freeing up engineers to handle other tasks. There was always more needed, and only so much time in the day to attempt it.

They'd docked with *Northwind* twelve hours and seventeen minutes ago. Finished transferring wounded four hours ago and turned the gravity systems back on. Knight Konicek and a crew were in *Marrakesh*'s flight bay, fabricating a plate to cover the hole in the near flank so they could seal it up.

In an emergency, there were plastic sheets that could be glued in place to hold air, but not for very long, spanning a space that big, as the outermost hole was several meters across, where about half of the energy had liberated directly on *Northwind*'s hull in that first instant.

Nyssa was mostly alone on the bridge. Right now, her best job was watching the inner portions of the system and identifying everything going on. *Northwind* had a lot of data, but nobody knew if it had gotten scrambled when the bridge was destroyed. And wouldn't until Bex and Glen could help wire up a few spans to let Nyssa access those datacores with her tools.

One hundred and eighty-three local ships had been identified and recorded. Most of them small, where wildcatters would nose up to a rock, then drill some holes in it and assay the interior. Nickel, iron, and carbon were fairly common, and useful, but someone finding something up in the platinum groups would be rich when they turned in their claim, and she was reading enough common and unencrypted traffic to understand that there'd been at least one good supernova in the past to seed this place with heavier stuff.

The kind that might even make this system profitable for civilians.

They called it Domnall, though that didn't apply to any of the planets or moons. Apparently, it was the name of the man who had first surveyed the system and convinced someone to move mining exploration ships out here.

Already, there was something of a base coming into being, docked next to that massive factory ship down where she would have expected the second planet to be orbiting, based on the amount of rubble.

It almost looked like some early celestial interaction had torn apart all of those small worlds closer in, possibly while evicting whatever larger planets might have originally formed in that range.

Just a navigational mess. And a scanner nightmare, as you had to broadcast constantly, then filter out a haze of noise reflecting off all the rubble.

However, it also let her sit quietly and listen. And copy a lot of audio traffic that appeared to be utterly mundane at the moment. *Marrakesh* had been upgraded with a whole third data-core dedicated entirely to Nyssa's needs, so space was cheap. No reason not to drink in the entire firehose. Someone might find it useful later. Or they could delete it after analysis.

Not her job.

Her job was surveillance. Watching that station come into being. About half-done, but they were building it like an onion in reverse. Core with life support and power. Then build a ring out as metal plate got smelted, processed, and shaped. Painfully slow, but it would create a self-contained economy as it went.

Nyssa even noted the presence of a freighter converted to nothing but hydroponics and aquaponics. Growing greens, fruit, and fish. Packed and stacked with equipment, selling produce to various ships and buying organic waste.

Someone was planning something big here, but doing it quietly. A mission years in the making. Quiet years. Build up a facility where nobody was watching. Out where *A'Zedi* wouldn't notice it.

Old enough to have perhaps predated the most recent war.

And Nyssa could see where a few megafreighters hauling grain in would turn this into something huge.

The *Wronlori* fleet had to be involved at some level, because a place like this would not have normally rated a half-dozen police cutters, even as search and rescue. A corporate overlord might have included one. Possibly two, while cutting costs at every corner.

This place wasn't cutting corners. It was growing like a pearl, around a grain of sand that was that factory ship.

What would it do to their plans if that ship were destroyed?

Nyssa so desperately wanted to convince Captain Boru that he should strike it, but that risked their own cover identity. If everyone assumed that *Marrakesh* was a simple Tactical Transport, they wouldn't pay attention, except to note how lucky the ship seemed to be.

Extremely lucky.

Destroying that factory might be pushing it.

Nyssa settled in and continued typing up notes that some future squadron commander could use to come in and thoroughly finish this place off.

It felt like the war needed such a thing.

25

Jocelyn studied the results. Ugly, but they hadn't taken the time to make it pretty.

Not when the steel plate in front of her was intended mostly as a bandage that could cover the wound until a proper shipyard could repair the damage.

She presumed that fully repairing it would involve debriding hull back at least four meters in any direction, then welding in a newly built section to replace it.

Later.

Captain Boru entering the flight deck caused Jocelyn to look up. *Roadrunner* was parked close and would carry the patch over. Senior Expert Rafferty, the Flight Deck boss, was standing in the hatch of his shuttle, waiting for her to finish this inspection and call it good.

Jocelyn shrugged and promised herself a nap when this was done. She'd been up for nearly twenty-four hours at this point, meditating a couple of times and fortified with coffee.

Nothing new in this business.

"Captain," she nodded as Boru stepped close.

Always, that unconscious glance down, seeing her more in the bodysuit she wore under this armor, like she'd been for more than a week. Appreciative glance.

"Checking on your needs, Konicek," he replied evenly.

Jocelyn kept herself from a flirtatious response. Business first. Other things later, even if Kaitlin had told her that the man wasn't all that into females.

Usually.

"We're ready to deploy this," she gestured to the deck plate. "Mounted from the outside, where it can cover the big hole, and be tack welded down until folks can seal it up from the inside with better welds and caulk. Since that team is finishing up the other hole now, Engineering should be able to hold atmosphere in about six hours."

He nodded, watching without comment. She waited, because there was something in his eyes. Something serious.

"Is the ship in good enough shape that we could give it a solid push?" he asked.

It took her a moment to process those words.

"Why?" Jocelyn finally asked.

"Two mines firing gave us a vector to look for *Northwind*," he replied. "And made it relatively easy to locate, even as dark as the ship is. *Marrakesh* isn't as hard to see from a distance, so someone looking this direction might be able to spot us. Especially if they knew which needle to start with. We've got the extra horsepower to carry *Northwind*, but I don't want to trigger the Ghostdrives because that will make us visible for many light-years. Rotary thrusters, however, could nudge us into a different orbit. I want to make it as hard as possible for that enemy commander."

"You expecting someone to locate us, sir?" she asked.

"I assume it," he nodded. "While you are repairing things, my job is to protect you and your crews as well as I can."

Jocelyn considered it and nodded.

"Nothing I've seen suggests that *Northwind* couldn't take it," she replied. "The damage is internal, but not particularly structural in nature. *Northwind* is really just a tapered cylinder, but I presume you aren't talking major thrust."

"That's correct," he agreed. "Gyros to turn us sideways, then rotary thrusters to push us up and out."

"When?" she demanded, thinking of the big plate at her feet.

"When you're ready for it," he replied, a grin in his eyes that didn't quite make it to his mouth. "You're in charge of this part of the operation, after all."

Jocelyn wanted to say something, but she was surrounded by her folks, and his. And he was keeping the subtext so perfectly innocent that she might have misread it.

"Four hours?" she asked. "That gets us out and completes this part of the mission. My engineers can work inside with gravity at that point, so they only need to brace for the initial jolt of thrust."

"It will be delicate, Konicek," he nodded. "Patient, because it's going to be something new for a lot of us. We'll work our way forward slowly. Carefully. Then get it all settled in comfortably."

Jocelyn almost blushed, parsing his words, but she'd been visually teasing the man for more than a week, so she supposed that it was only fair he teased her back.

And how he went about it.

She grinned anyway. If nothing else, here was somebody she could dance with verbally, when that wasn't all that common, either. Intelligent man, but also *smart*.

"I'll do my part, Captain," she countered. "The rest, I guess, will be up to you."

That little flair in his eyes was the frosting on top, as far as she was concerned.

"Looking forward to it, Knight," he grinned as well, then turned and departed without another word. Or even a glance back, but she had work to do.

"Okay, people," Jocelyn called. "We're good here. Flight Boss, you're on."

Time to go plug *Northwind*.

26

Padraig couldn't help the spring in his step. And he didn't normally even like women.

Jocelyn Konicek, however…

He could see making an exception.

The bridge was quiet when he arrived. Nyssa was on duty, looking positively shaggy because she might not have buzzed her skull to the minimum regulation hair length in several days. It was almost long enough to measure, but he didn't mention that.

She'd immediately cut it too short as a dare.

One of these days, Padraig was going to have to authorize her to shave and polish it smooth. She hadn't requested it formally, but others had gossiped.

Whatever it took to keep Nyssa Taggart at the peak of her game.

Nyssa was the only officer present, but that was a result of his current standing orders that all training and recertifications be delayed to make bodies available for whatever tasks were needed.

Andrea Whelan was watch-sitting the Helm, next to Nyssa. Command Expert. Coxswain of the Boat. Senior enlisted crew member aboard.

The woman could handle any job on the ship, including his.

Padraig still wasn't sure how he'd managed to get her, let alone keep her, when there were Ships-of-the-Line out there that didn't have a Coxswain as good.

Not that he was about to tempt the gods of the fleet by mentioning that out loud.

Padraig slid into his station. Nyssa looked up querulously.

"I'm taking command, Radio," he said simply.

"You have command," she nodded.

Padraig turned to Andrea. Brown hair. Light skin. Hazel eyes, which were always odd to look at, since brown was so much more common. Petite woman, verging on tiny. Just barely met minimum height and weight standards to remain on active duty, in spite of being in her mid-forties.

She made up for it in personality.

"Sir?" Andrea asked in a sidelong kind of voice that stretched three letters into several syllables.

Like she knew he was up to no good.

"When *Roadrunner* completes its mission, we're going to rotate the combined mass, Cox," he nodded. "Then accelerate slowly, pushing the two of us up and out on a new vector at odds with the current trajectory we matched to dock with *Northwind*."

She was considering her words delicately, from the way her lips moved. Padraig waited.

"Down would be better," she offered. "Fewer stars to back-light us that way, when seen from deeper in."

Padraig nodded. Andrea might not be—quite—as good a navigator as Zarah Halloran, but that gap was measured in millimeters.

"You plot it," he ordered. "We have several hours until we can do anything significant, so use that time to refine things, then bring Halloran up to date and decide who will be at Helm when we do it. Questions?"

"Anywhere far, sir?" Andrea asked.

"Away," he shook his head. "Slowly and carefully. I want anyone looking at that original vector we were on to miss us.

Maybe not for long, but every little bit helps, when we're hiding like this."

"Roger that, sir," she nodded, then went to work.

Padraig called up his own screens and pulled open a report on logistics consumption from Chief Jackstadt, having had a chance to inventory what could be salvaged from *Northwind* to add to *Marrakesh*'s current stores.

The paperwork never ceased, even on the most dangerous missions.

27

Kaitlin hadn't had much to do on this mission. Walker and his people tended to be a self-contained lot. Not insular, but not really out needing to bother Padraig's crew. And right now, everybody available was heads down on some repair task, with her mostly providing a central point of communications for folks to find one another.

Mother hen, if you will. Helped that she was older than everyone else, so they would defer some.

Her board rang as she sat and monitored things.

"Forward pod. Lynch."

"Sir, this is Bex Magorian. I've got a bit of an issue here and not really sure who I should drag in to help."

Kaitlin nodded. One of Nyssa's people. One on the edge of knowing the truth, but not all of it.

Not like Kaitlin did.

"What do you need, Bex?" Kaitlin asked.

"Muscle, as much as anything, sir," Bex replied. "Got something that needs to be removed, but I can't get in there with anything useful to pry it sideways and can't use much force because I have something really delicate right behind it that I don't want to risk breaking. Need someone with muscles, but also a really high security clearance."

Kaitlin nodded. Muscles aplenty around here. Security clearances, as well, but most of *Marrakesh*'s crew probably didn't rate high enough, since Kaitlin knew where Magorian was working at the moment. And Bex was a small woman. Strawberry blonde throwback who looked more like a citizen of the *Enlightened Tyranny of Traisa* than an *A'Zedi* citizen.

"You take a quick potty break, Magorian," Kaitlin instructed the youngster. "I'll be along in a few."

"You, sir?"

"Me," Kaitlin nodded to herself.

"Roger that."

Kaitlin killed the line and dialed a number.

"Gilroy."

"Denny, where is your spare wrench?" Kaitlin asked.

Denny was her first assistant. Ship's Docker. A powerful man who also did puzzle stacking games at galactic expert level, with good *feng shui* to his visible tattoos.

And a one-hundred-and-forty centimeter adjustment wrench that could do damned near any task Denny needed.

"Should be in my locker," he replied after a moment. "What's up?"

"Need to borrow it to help Magorian move something," Kaitlin replied.

"You break it, you're buying me a new one," he said warily.

"Deal, you scoundrel," she laughed. "You didn't buy the one in your hands right now."

"True."

She cut the line and went looking for the toolbox that Denny had moved onto the shuttle and latched down. The engineers had wanted to object, until Kaitlin had pointed out that not letting Denny's people store tools here meant that they had to borrow ones from Walker's crew instead.

At that point, everyone had shut up.

Adjustment wrench. What a lovely euphemism. She'd seen Denny throw it like a tomahawk at Albany. Or get under it with enough torque to bow his usual wrench by almost a millimeter out of true.

She grabbed it, pushed the button once to confirm that it was fully charged, and headed down to where she could cross over to *Northwind*.

She found Bex Magorian at a hatch marked *Secured*. For a ship like *Northwind*, that meant a whole extra level of security above and beyond what most sailors ever encountered in their entire careers.

Even Kaitlin, before she'd been seduced back to duty and given *Marrakesh* as a prize.

Kaitlin was one hundred and sixty centimeters tall, and felt like she towered over the tinier Magorian. Bex typed a seventeen-digit code into the hatch to open it, and Kaitlin followed her through.

The air in here had a staleness that the filters hadn't been able to clear. That hint of old smoke you got when wires overloaded and cooked. About half the lights didn't work, in a random pattern, but they were also exactly one deck below the primary bridge, where starlight would be visible if you entered.

"How bad was the damage, Bex?" Kaitlin asked as they turned a corner and stopped at a hatch requiring a twenty-two-digit password this time.

"Overloads managed to blow the fuses so fast that they jumped the gap and continued," the woman said in a quiet voice. "I've never seen a single power surge do so much damage. It actually welded plates in place when it grounded to the hull."

"And the datacore behind it?" Kaitlin pressed as the hatch opened.

"I'm hoping that it was sufficiently insulated, boss," Bex shrugged. "Won't know until we get there."

The room was austere. Banks of computers, slid in like pizza boxes on rails, covering three of the walls.

Northwind's brains.

About half of them were dark. One entire stack had obviously been fried, from the smoke that had stained the metal itself on the outside. Others blinked in ways that suggested serious psychological damage, if you could give a starship a concussion.

She'd had a few in her time.

Bex knelt next to a toolbox that had been stuck to the floor and closed. Finer work, instead of plumber's wrenches and such.

Playing with delicate electronics, when Denny was repairing fuel lines by ripping out damaged pipe manually and welding in new stuff.

"Here," Bex said, grabbing a pocketflash and aiming it into a hole behind a plate she had removed.

Kaitlin squatted down, then went ahead and knelt. About a shoebox for height and width. Enough to get one arm in, but not two.

"Got a diagram?" Kaitlin asked after studying the hole for a moment.

Bex handed her a repair tablet with the room notes on it. And a checkered red and white border indicating the level of security clearance necessary to even know this document existed, let alone to read it.

"Plate seventeen is supposed to come out," Bex explained. "All the bolts are out and in my pocket. Can't get it to move, and I don't have anything that can get under it and not damage the corewall itself."

Kaitlin grabbed the light and moved herself around to look better.

"Crap," she muttered.

"Sir?"

"Faraday cage works both ways," Kaitlin replied. "It doesn't look like it jumped that gap, so it had to ground into the uninsulated parts of the frame instead."

"Worried about that," Bex said. "Not sure if I should ask the captain to send a team down here with a cutting laser and open up the wall beside you to start detaching things. Risk there is that the ship will not fly without them. Even with the secondary bridge mostly intact."

"Mostly?" Kaitlin looked up sharply.

"They came within thirty-seven centimeters of joining the primary bridge," Bex nodded. "I measured it. Lucky for them, it also missed the chamber with all their computers, or they'd have probably had to immediately abandon ship and be captured. I know Squire Taggart wants me to confirm that all this stuff works, but I can't justify taking the whole ship permanently off-line to do that. Not yet. That's where you come in, sir."

Kaitlin nodded and checked it again. Then she zoomed in closer on the tablet.

She wasn't likely to break Denny's wrench, but this would still be hinky. That was a technical term with engineers and dockers.

"Sir?" Bex asked when Kaitlin grunted.

"You hold the light here," Kaitlin said, handing it to her and pointing it just so.

Kaitlin shifted to her right to get her stronger left hand into the gap, wrench first. Then she put it down and felt in and around that plate, letting her fingertips be her eyes.

Her finger didn't fit, so she pulled her hand out and dialed the crescent wrench portion down to a fine chisel tip. Maybe one side of an eight millimeter wrench.

That got cammed into place as best she could, then Kaitlin thumbed the button to torque it down into the available space and grab on.

Kaitlin nodded once to herself and drew a breath, holding it then releasing slowly. Second breath in, she grabbed the wrench with both hands and flexed upwards with her back as she blew out.

It was like lifting *Northwind* itself. And it kinda was, since that plate didn't want to come out.

Stubborn.

Kaitlin Lynch was more stubborn. She growled at it. Leaned hard into it. Got her butt involved.

And landed on her ass when it broke loose and she flew into the air suddenly.

Bex was standing over her when she stopped blinking.

"You okay?" the woman asked.

Kaitlin shook her head to check. Nothing rattled loose.

No more loose than normal.

"Did I get it?" Kaitlin asked.

Bex was holding a small plate by two fingers on one corner.

"Don't touch it," the woman said. "Really hot."

Kaitlin nodded and climbed back to her feet slowly. Might be bruises tomorrow, but she had enough ass to cushion things appropriately.

They knelt. Bex stuck Denny's spare wrench into the hole and backed out bolts quickly, slipping them into a pocket while Kaitlin watched and recovered.

"Here goes nothing," Bex said, putting the wrench down and reaching an arm in.

A moment later, she pulled out a box about the size of a brick, trailing wires that got unplugged.

"Does this officially make me a spy, boss?" Bex asked, her face somewhere between ironic grin and concerned grimace.

"Probably," Kaitlin nodded. "But you already know what *Marrakesh* is about, and know how to keep your mouth shut, or Nyssa would have had you transferred to another boat by now. Just remember to keep your mouth shut. Captain knows. Commander Messier. Me. And now you."

"Glen has a pretty good idea," Bex countered.

"Tell him to keep quiet, too, then," Kaitlin ordered. "The repair depot folks know that we get sent on hinky missions, but they don't need to know just how hinky. Understood?"

"Aye, sir," Bex nodded.

Kaitlin watched Bex open the toolbox and pull out a similar-looking brick, plugging the two together and pushing a red button on top.

"This will take about three hours to copy everything, according to Squire Taggart," Bex said. "I'm ready for lunch."

"I think I'll join you, Bex," Kaitlin said. "Let's find someplace quiet and talk business."

They rose and made their way out of the chamber.

Bex Magorian wasn't as smart as Nyssa Taggart, but nobody else was, either. Kaitlin could see the young woman stepping up, though.

Padraig would need all the help he could get, if they were going to keep doing these sorts of missions.

28

———

Nyssa had left Captain Boru a note requesting a meeting. He'd seen it when he woke up and sent a reply with a time. She'd been sitting in his office when he arrived after eating.

Everyone else was pulling crazy hours working on repairs, but he'd specifically kept her separate, while he generally supervised things.

Yet another one of those little conspiracies that only the two of them shared.

He settled in behind his desk and watched her. Nyssa had spent a lot of the morning framing her words.

The silence stretched, but that was fine.

"I have been studying the interior of this system extensively, sir," she finally began, having false started twice after realizing she'd already moved too far forward in her explanation and needed to start at the beginning.

"What conclusions have you been able to come to, Squire?" he asked simply.

Nyssa nodded. That was why she liked working for him. She could start in one place and he could make the logical and intuitive leaps to keep up with her, even when she wasn't entirely sure where she was going.

"This station will be, at minimum another year in construction, sir," she replied. "They've been working for several years so far, but started extremely small. That factory ship and perhaps a dozen wildcatters at the beginning. More have come along as either word has gotten out on the *Wronlori* side, or they've hired civilians to work here. None of it has any military appearance that I've been able to detect. And that doesn't make sense, sir."

There. She'd said it. Admitted to the confusion that had irritated the living shit out of her.

There should be answers. Why couldn't she find them?

His smile warmed her.

"It's all a Potemkin village, Taggart," he said.

blorp...

"Sir?"

"It's all fake," he nodded. "They are building up this place and making it look like a simple civilian mining colony. You have, however, noted any number of crucial abnormalities that don't add up. Too many police cutters, for one. Then there is that damnable minefield that nearly killed *Northwind*."

"What does it mean, sir?" Nyssa asked.

It felt like he'd seen something she'd missed. Something important.

"Someone funded that factory ship," Captain Boru said, ticking off points on his hand as he named them. "That minefield is extremely expensive to put in place, and would have absolutely no value to a mining colony like this one. Compare it to Varfelis Station."

"There is hardly any comparison, sir," she offered. "That one was almost a wild west area, where pirates were largely free to roam, kept at a distance only because the station itself was so heavily armed."

"And have you seen any such armaments on the factory ship or the station they are building?" he pressed.

"None, which makes no sense," she admitted.

"I'm willing to bet that they're there, Squire," he smiled.

"Hidden, like we did at Varfelis. Blow off panels and suddenly you have a tremendous amount of firepower to slaughter some fool pirate who got too close. Same with those cutters. I'm willing to bet you a bronze, ten ducat coin, that they are also Q-ships, designed to wolfpack on some pirate with particle cannons far in excess of their hull rating."

"Why?"

"Intelligence was concerned enough to send *Northwind*. They wanted to find out what was going on here," he explained. "Ship got into serious trouble, but nothing happened when those mines fired. I suspect that only a portion of the folks in charge around here are aware that the military authorities are behind everything. And I'm only guessing, mind you, but that makes the most sense to me, having read your various reports and analyses."

"Did they think they got a kill?" she asked. "Why not confirm?"

"Maybe they honestly missed it," he shrugged. "Maybe they saw us the moment we arrived and sent a ship racing to summon help. You've been closely monitoring the Aetherial channels, but haven't detected anything out of the ordinary. But how many ships have departed since we arrived?"

"Seventeen," she nodded, feeling better that some of the pieces were starting to make sense. "Would they send a courier to bring back a cruiser? Or a Leviathan?"

"Don't know," he offered. "I do know that we're in better shape to run at high speed if we must. And we can right now, if we withdraw everyone from the derelict in a hurry."

"Are they lulling us to sleep in the meantime?" Nyssa asked.

"That's why you've remained on detached duty from the repair work, Squire," he nodded. "And I've made it a point to remain close in case I need to take operational command back from Nylund, which would happen if an enemy warship showed up."

"Why haven't you told anyone, sir?" she asked, concerned.

"Because I can't prove anything right now, Taggart," he said with a grimace. "Not until something happens. Presumably, even those cutters, if they are armed like that, don't think they are enough to attack us with certainty. Until we deploy the depot, *Marrakesh* would look like a normal Line Cruiser, if someone was watching from a distance, so maybe we've fooled them, as well."

"Should we be preparing the crew to abandon *Northwind* on short notice?" she asked.

"Scuttling charges were one of the first things I asked Knight Konicek to repair," he answered. "The ship can be blown in place whenever we need it. I understand that your folks have recovered most of the intelligence data *Northwind* had accumulated before the minefield. Technically, we could flee right now and the mission would be a success, as we've gotten the ship's crew to safety and the data."

"Then why don't we, sir?" she asked.

"Because they might have honestly missed us," he replied. "We might be able to get the Ghostdrives and rotary thrusters to the point that we could move the ship someplace where the locals couldn't find us, which would give Nylund's people time to do a better repair job than the hacking and patching they've done so far. I'd like to bring the ship home, and not just the crew."

"Oh," she said, seeing all the wheels and circles to his thinking finally. "And if a *Wronlori* force shows up?"

"If they're small, we might fight," he said bluntly. "I doubt that we'll have such an opportunity, though. If they did see us and think we're a cruiser, they'll bring a squadron or something. *Marrakesh* looks a lot more dangerous than she is. At least from that distance."

"Is there anything I can do to prepare?" Nyssa asked.

He paused and she watched his eyes flicker back and forth rapidly, like he was scanning some screen at high speed.

"Varfelis Station," he said suddenly, eyes locking onto hers like a predator about to pounce.

"Sir?"

"You did something to that one transport, Taggart," he

continued. "Locked them out of their own systems, then fired their cannon at their friends."

"*Black Albatross*, Captain," Nyssa nodded, remembering.

Grocery store ship with an automated ordering system that had been simple enough that her new tools allowed her to break in and then step sideways into the rest of their systems.

And lock the crew out of most of them by downgrading everybody else's accounts.

"That one," he agreed. "What could you do to *Northwind*, given time?"

Nyssa jolted backwards so hard that her shoulder blades might have bruises from the chair tomorrow.

What could she do?

Patrol version of a standard Line Cruiser, just as *Marrakesh* was the Tactical Transport version. Less firepower, because guns and missiles required crew to operate.

And *Northwind* was a spy version of a Patrol Cruiser, so even smaller crew.

She struggled for a moment, then went ahead and pulled up the tablet she'd taken to carrying with her, from where she'd rested it leaning against his desk while she waited.

One turret forward. Heavy twin particle cannon. *Marrakesh* had two and most Line Cruisers had four. Same four lighter particle cannons on the corners for defense. Same twin railgun pulsars.

Missiles...there. Two tubes down each flank instead of *Marrakesh*'s three and a Line's four.

Nyssa calculated, thankful that Captain Boru sat and waited.

"Fully remote, sir?" she asked.

"If it can't escape, I'd rather not allow *Wronlori* to capture it, Squire," he nodded. "That includes any crew."

"I could probably wire a few systems to let Maddox Nevin control things from here," she offered. "Possibly set up on their secondary bridge to keep the controllers more clearly delineated."

"Hold that thought," the captain said, then opened the hatch with his controls.

"Nevin!" he called.

"Here, sir," Maddox replied.

"Turn over command and join me," Captain Boru ordered.

Nyssa checked that her screen wasn't showing anything too important and waited.

Maddox entered a moment later.

"Sir?"

"Sit," Boru said. "Got a scenario for you, Gunner."

Nyssa watched Maddox settle warily. Ship's Gunner. Fourth generation sailor but first generation as an officer. Sharp and aggressive, which was what you wanted in his job.

Nice, though. He'd settled into a role more as a big brother than anything, though he wasn't nearly as big as the two she'd grown up with.

Safe to be around. That helped a lot, when she was so much younger than the other officers present. And most of the crew.

"Taggart might be able to take remote control of weapons systems on *Northwind*, Nevin," the captain began. "No crew, so nobody to repair things if anything breaks, but functional. With me so far?"

"Aye, sir," Maddox nodded, glancing over at her.

"If somebody dropped out of Ghost-space and wanted to fight, how hard would it be for you or one of your people to handle all of *Northwind*'s weapons like that?" Captain Boru asked.

"Can they jam our signals?" Maddox asked, turning to look directly at her.

"No," Nyssa replied simply.

He nodded and turned back to the captain.

"Guns will be fine, but I'll need to inspect them more closely, sir," Maddox replied. "Something will overheat, and I won't have the people to adjust things on the fly, so they'll have to fall out of firing cycle until they recover. Same with missiles. We can load the trays now, but the whole reason you have a crew down there is that things break. Lines kink. Missiles wobble on the tray or fall off. Not as many tubes, but entropy reduces us to probably one by the third salvo. Longer if nobody's shooting at *Northwind*. Shorter if they panic and hammer us hard early."

He fell silent and Nyssa watched Captain Boru weigh the odds.

"Nevin, you detach from all duty and immediately go over and inspect *Northwind*'s weapon systems," he said. "I can't imagine what force mix *Wronlori* might send after us, so I can't be sure what missile load-out to use. Give me an even mix of Sixes and Nines. *Marrakesh* can focus on Threes if we need to kill a Leviathan. Check in with me or Taggart when you finish your inspection for more orders. Dismissed."

"Aye, sir." Maddox bounced up out of his chair and out the hatch almost in a single step.

Captain Boru turned back to look at her.

"You wire it so that he can fight *Northwind* from the bridge," Captain said simply. "We'll put Kellen Doherty in charge of *Marrakesh*'s guns initially, also from the bridge, so Maddox can give her orders when he needs to coordinate things. Don't try to hack into someone's systems unless we can confirm that they are civilian. Instead, if trouble erupts, I need you making sure that nobody has snuck around behind us, outside of Aetherial scanner range, and is lying in wait on a game trail for us to blast by, thinking we've escaped. Questions?"

"None at present, sir," Nyssa said, feeling much better.

That niggling concern at the back of her head had abated somewhat. Fallen into a checklist of other concerns that were more what she was used to.

Keep watch. Secure the electronic perimeter. Enable remote access.

"I'll need permission and certain passwords from Commander Kingston, sir," Nyssa remembered.

Northwind was a spy ship. Things would be as secured over there as she generally kept them over here.

"Make a list and I'll pull her aside," he nodded. "Excellent work, by the way, Taggart. Keep it up."

Nyssa blushed in spite of herself.

"Dismissed," he ordered and she rose, drawing a heavy breath.

It was a long list of things, but she had a plan now.

29

———

Padraig had remained almost exclusively aboard *Marrakesh* during this operation, mostly so he was always available and ready if something happened. Similarly, Artemis Kingston had stayed aboard *Northwind* for the most part, providing local expertise as strangers boarded and needed to do things.

He met her at the line separating the ships with a smile.

"Permission to come aboard, Captain?" she asked.

"Welcome, Commander," he replied. "I've set us up in a nearby conference room and folks know where to find you if they need."

They got there and he made sure she got a large mug of coffee. He'd seen how worn she'd looked when they'd arrived. If anything, she looked worse now, but that was transitioning from despair to grinding work, trying to save the ship she'd inherited when Captain Harrington had been killed.

Just like it would have been, had Chance suddenly been in charge of a partial derelict, deep behind enemy lines.

He let her sit and sip for a moment.

"Okay, I needed that," she announced.

"Thought you might," Padraig nodded. "I would like to ask

your permission to do a few highly unorthodox things, Artemis," he began simply.

"I'm only a Commander, Captain," she replied.

"Acting Captain in Command of *Northwind*, Kingston," he replied. "My peer. Your ship. Your decisions."

She blinked at that like an owl suddenly wakened by noise. He nodded and let her process.

"What's up, Captain?" she asked.

"Call me Padraig," he replied. "Peers. As to what's up, I need to brief you on a few things that do not leave this room. Understood?"

She nodded warily.

"*Northwind* is a spy ship," Padraig began. "I'm aware of that, because my boss filled me in with a great deal more information than most officers would ever get."

"And your boss is?" she probed, turning serious.

"Mariami Gelashvili," Padraig told her. "Permanent First Secretary, Civil Service, *A'Zedi* Intelligence Operations on Horwin. *Marrakesh* is also a spy ship, but a different kind. We undertake undercover operations based on mission modules and need, while looking like a simple Tactical Transport."

He waited as she blinked once, processing all that.

"And they sent you here because...?"

"She also thinks we're lucky," Padraig grinned. "And you know how superstitious sailors can be. I've had luck. Trying not to use it all up, but this situation is serious."

"Extremely, Cap—Padraig."

He smiled at her.

"During a previous operation, my Radio officer was able to override an enemy civilian vessel and take command of their weapons systems, Artemis," he continued. "Introducing chaos when that ship opened fire on their nominal allies in the middle of battle. I'd like to do something similar here."

"What?" she asked, back to confused.

"Program *Northwind* to let my Gunner fight your vessel from my bridge, Captain," Padraig said. "With all your crew withdrawn to safety on *Marrakesh*. All this presumes that bad guys show up and start trouble. We're only a few days from possibly being able to run like hell, so this might be overt paranoia on my part. I'd prefer to never have to put something like this into play, but I'd rather have it and not need it, than need it and not have it."

"My Coxswain, Katsuya Kuchi, was previously a Gunnery watch-sitter," she said. "He probably knows those systems best. And better than your Gunner will, Padraig."

Padraig nodded.

"I wasn't presuming that your crew would be sufficiently recovered to be involved, Artemis," he said with a smile. "But I'd be happy to sit him on my bridge with Armiger Nevin in overall command. If this happens before *Northwind* can escape, I'd like to use the ship up entirely in battle, possibly wreaking as much havoc and damage around here as I can. My Radio officer, Nyssa Taggart, tells me that this appears to be a secret base being built quietly by the *Wronlori* military for some future shenanigans. Which is presumably why you were sent out."

"It is," Artemis agreed. "We had gathered up a tremendous amount of signals intelligence for analysis. I gave Taggart's people the codes they needed to gain access and copy everything. You're wanting override codes for the full ship?"

"If you'll allow it, Captain," Padraig replied formally. "That's your ship. Your command, however temporary and situational. I'm asking for permission to possibly destroy it in the line of duty, but I cannot command you in that task."

"If someone shows up and *Northwind* cannot flee, my orders were to destroy the vessel," she reminded him. "And possibly the crew, depending on the situation, as many of us should not be subjected to interrogation by *Wronlori* Intelligence."

"I don't plan on letting them, Captain," he smiled. "What I'd like to do is set up a few surprises."

"In that case, I am happy to help, Captain?" she smiled back.

Padraig leaned forward and started explaining it.

30

Maddox hadn't worked with *Northwind*'s Coxswain all that much, as the man had been busy aft helping the folks repair Engineering up until now.

Nobody had expected to need the weapons on a derelict.

Until now.

Command Expert Kuchi was a regular guy. Career enlisted who'd had no interest in any sort of commission. Maddox knew the type. Andrea Whelan was similar. Old enough to be his dad, with a calm, phlegmatic approach to things.

Except that he'd risen to Second-in-Command of *Northwind* by virtue of casualties and injuries.

"Why are you so certain, Armiger?" the man asked as they inspected the missile storage racks.

Big metal tubes designed to feed a missile in automatically, once someone decided the launch order and type desired.

Then sat and waited for something to go wrong with the launch sequence. Kinked lines. Impact jarring something out of true.

Normally, you had a crew handy with big tools to fix it immediately.

That wouldn't be an option.

Even if someone showed up in the next five minutes, standing orders were to fully evacuate *Northwind* with no exceptions. Abandon ship so *Marrakesh* could run, because *Northwind* was stuck here for a few more days at a dead minimum.

And that assumed everything went just right with the repairs.

Maddox considered the question.

"Captain Boru has a gut feeling, Cox," he replied. "And those have kept us alive more than once. He wants us to be able to punch somebody in the mouth if they show up."

"We hardly ever ran missile drills, Gunner," Kuchi replied. "This was not that ship. Hell, I'm surprised that they even included them in the design, except that we're based on a Patrol Cruiser and that's how they come off the dock."

"Should we not trust these trays?" Maddox asked, tapping one that had a big Six ready to be loaded.

Anti-matter thruster at the rear could generate a lot of acceleration, given time. Front end split lengthwise into six equal parts when the missile reached burnout, spreading some to increase your chances of a hit. And give enemy gunners more things to try to stop with their own particle cannon.

"I'd say you were safe with one reload salvo," the man nodded seriously. "Past that, your chances go down rapidly. Nobody has tested the lines to see if they torqued any when shit went sideways. Wasn't important in the grand scheme of keeping the survivors alive. How much time do we have here?"

"Time? I have no idea," Maddox replied. "And we don't really have the bodies to do this, because that requires pulling the experts off more important things, which slows the recovery down."

He paused as a rude idea crept up and bit him on the ass.

"You got something?" Kuchi asked.

"Maybe," Maddox replied, reaching for the comm line.

"Bridge. Taggart."

"Nyssa, is the Captain available?" Maddox asked.

"He's mobile. Stand by," she said.

Moving around the ship somewhere. Normal for Captain Boru, who liked to touch things and talk to people, instead of talking on the comm and reviewing reports from his office.

"Nevin, what do you have?" Captain Boru was on the line suddenly.

"Requesting permission to use up resources at a prodigious rate and in a most wasteful manner, sir," Maddox replied, feeling his tones get formal.

This was the sort of phrase that got read back to you at a court martial later, if you screwed up. Or pissed off the wrong flag officer.

"How wasteful, sailor?" Captain Boru asked sternly.

"Albany, sir," Maddox said with a grin in his voice. "Got a lot of missiles here and we're not sure we can trust the automated launch systems to work efficiently in battle. I'm proposing what we did to that Leviathan. Only, with twenty missiles instead of one. Empty the magazines save for missiles in the tubes directly as a full salvo of Nines to add to the general chaos of a mass launch."

"If you think you can program that sort of thing, Nevin," Captain replied.

"Negative, sir," Maddox almost laughed. "Permission to drag in Halloran and Taggart. They've already got the tools handy."

There was enough of a pause that Maddox could look at the disbelief on Kuchi's face, then the captain finally spoke.

"Go for it, Gunner," he ordered with a laugh. "Leave everything with self-destruct circuits on a timer if we don't end up using them."

"Should we also program a deadman timer to send them down after that factory station once they lose contact with *Marrakesh*, sir?" Maddox asked.

"Negative, Armiger," the man came down hard. "That's a civilian operation that has offered us no threat at present. Aim them for deep space instead."

"Understood, sir," Maddox said, sobering and cutting the line.

They might be the enemy, but Captain had hard and fast rules on certain things. Until somebody over there threw the first punch, *Marrakesh* would ignore them.

"You gonna explain all that?" Kuchi asked, gesturing with both hands to encompass pretty much everything.

"We're going to reprogram the missile control systems, Cox," Maddox smiled. "Then soft launch them without a firing signal, letting them drift in space in a cloud around us, slowly expanding over time as everyone moves. Our Radio officer is capable of controlling them remotely, so we can identify a target and aim things at them from all sides. Hell of a surprise when we did it to *Sundering Wrath*."

"That was the Leviathan you chased off?" the man asked.

"That was the Leviathan we nearly killed in single combat before they ran like hell from us, Coxswain," Maddox said seriously.

"Gotcha, sir," Kuchi nodded. "What do we need here?"

"You and me need to go talk to a couple of really scary-smart ladies."

31

Jocelyn was in her EVA armor, inspecting the work above *Northwind*'s stern as the team inside slowly brought the rotary thrusters on line and began testing them. Not even a tenth of one percent power, but they'd done this three times so far and seemed to have located and fixed all the leaks.

Hack job, through and through, but Boru had been correct that the most important thing they could do would be to move the ship into deep space, away from the Domnall system. Even then, deploying the depot would be risky, but that was part of the reason she'd taken this job, instead of something safe and dull at a starbase drydock.

Predictable was another word for mind-numbing. Soul-crushing.

Yuck.

"EVA-1, stand by for power," Squire Taggart relayed on the closed channel.

Somehow, the woman had managed to lock a communications laser onto Jocelyn's suit that let them talk without broadcasting any signal. Couldn't handle too many people moving around, but Jocelyn had already ordered everyone to work inside the ship, only walking outside—directly on the hull itself—when absolutely necessary.

The cloud of angry hornets asleep around her was always in the back of Jocelyn's mind.

Captain Boru was serious about protecting them. And willing to go completely junkyard dog in the process.

She felt safer, knowing what he had done, but it still made this a hazard zone for navigation.

None of the missiles were visible to the naked eye, but she could see every one of them if she closed her eyes and imagined.

"Standing by for power, *Marrakesh*," Jocelyn replied evenly.

The two ships had separated for this test, just in case something went wrong. *Marrakesh* wasn't terribly far away in astronomical terms, but not close in case *Northwind* suddenly began spiraling or something.

Same reason Jocelyn was the only person outside, and she was above the stern and off a bit to one side, closer to *Marrakesh*.

Things might go wrong.

Below her, Jocelyn watched the rotary thrusters begin to glow, like candles in the window on a dark night.

"Flow appears clean and stable," Jocelyn reported, knowing that Taggart would route her words over to Walker and Thalia, as they monitored things from *Northwind*'s secondary bridge, which had become primary once it was clear how much effort it would take to even begin to repair the other one.

Later, when the ship got home safe.

Northwind wasn't going anywhere with this test. All they were doing was confirming that the systems worked end-to-end. Later, they'd review sensor logs and maybe put enough power through to actually change the drift from what *Marrakesh* had imparted a week ago.

Repair work was done in small pieces, getting this system rock solid before moving on to the next one. They had the people to do it right the first time, but that meant patching and hacking enough to fly.

Not to make it pretty.

Northwind would be a year in dock getting pretty again. Assuming that they didn't end up scrapping her once folks back home could crawl over everything with micrometers.

"EVA-1, this is Taggart, return to base immediately," the comm suddenly spoke. "I am declaring an emergency."

32

___

Nyssa watched hard. Close. Measured the signals from the inner system to *Marrakesh* with a steady hand. The light-speed lag to the factory station at the heart of the system was just over seven hours at present, and growing slowly longer as the two ships had inertia outwards.

It would take years to matter appreciably, but the vector was correct.

It was the Aetherial scanners that mattered. Even at maximum acceleration through regular space, it would take weeks for someone to get to them.

On Ghostdrives, it was measured in minutes. At most.

"EVA-1, stand by for power," Nyssa said, watching the feed from *Northwind*.

It wasn't that she didn't trust Mister Nylund and his people, but they weren't used to skulking, so she had shut down all external signals and spoke directly to Knight Konicek herself via a laser signal that would not be detectable at any range.

"Standing by for power, *Marrakesh*," Konicek replied.

Nyssa really enjoyed working with the woman. Starkly professional when she was on duty. Something of a goof otherwise. Knew some great dirty jokes.

And gossip suggested that she and the Captain might be a bit closer than one would normally expect. Nyssa hoped so. Captain Boru needed someone.

"*Northwind*, you are go for power up," Nyssa relayed. "Spotter is on station and observing."

"Roger that," Commander Kingston replied. "Powering up now."

Nyssa didn't have anything that could see the ship's rotary thrusters directly. Konicek's suit camera was pointed at deep space as the woman watched from the side. Still, she had echoed Kingston's controls through to her board with another laser.

Fuel feeds on and confirmed. Ignition and temperature stable.

Nyssa didn't really understand the deep details of what was happening, but Zarah was flying today and nodding as she watched the results on her own board. Others were calm as well.

"Flow appears clean and stable," Konicek announced.

Nyssa relayed and watched. All the dials and gauges seemed within normal bounds, and nobody was raising their voice.

A ping on her board caused Nyssa to shut down everything else.

The Aetherial scanners had just detected an inbound ship at extreme range.

No, scratch that. Three signals flying in tight formation.

Military tight, because Nyssa had studied folks at Varfelis Station enough to understand that civilians took a much looser approach to such things.

Even the pirates hadn't stayed that close together when flying in Ghost-space.

Nyssa opened the rocker and brought the ship to alert status in a single, fluid motion. Captain Boru had given her strict and specific instructions for a situation like this.

"EVA-1, this is Taggart, return to base immediately," Nyssa told Knight Konicek. "I am declaring an emergency."

She cut the line and ignored the woman. Bex would be watching. Or Glen. Someone else, because Nyssa was locked onto the feed.

"Radio?" Captain Boru asked calmly.

"Your screen two, sir," she said, sending her feed to everyone on the ship. "Enemy warship squadron inbound."

There wasn't anything else that could be.

"Acknowledged, Radio," he said. "All hands, you will immediately vacate *Northwind*. Repeat, vacate *Northwind* and return to *Marrakesh*. Do not stop for anything, as we have enemy vessels inbound. Helm, get us docked to Northwind immediately."

Medium FTL. Mark Four and change at present. Four light-years per hour.

The best *Marrakesh* had ever sustained had been just above Mark Six when fleeing that Leviathan. Captain seemed to think that Six point Five was possible, given the current state of the ship.

How fast could someone give chase?

"Helm, moving to dock now," Zarah called. "All hands stand by for maneuvers."

There weren't many people currently aboard *Northwind*. Captain Boru had laid down the rules and overruled even Mister Nylund for this one.

Luckily.

Three ships. Tight formation. High speed approach, aimed more or less directly at Domnall Station. Or whatever they called that factory. Depending on who was talking, they had about a dozen names for it, ranging from an alphanumeric to a couple of pretty ribald ones.

"Radio, time to intercept?" the captain called.

Nyssa did the math quickly.

"Twenty-two minutes to arrival at the factory station, sir," she said. "Best flight time from there is under thirty seconds, depending on their path."

"Helm, assume they know where we are and will vector down onto us directly," he called. "Plot me a course that takes maximum advantage of *Northwind* and her minefield. Gunnery teams, stand by to engage. Now would be a good time to take a potty break and get into suits. Wardroom, expect to be feeding people at stations until notified."

Nyssa nodded at all of it. She wouldn't say it was old hat by now, but there was a certain level of comfort that Captain Boru had reduced it almost to a checklist.

Trouble was coming to dinner.

33

———

Chance had kept a low profile for the most part, spending a lot of time down in the infirmary helping Elsy, because she'd kept her EMT certifications fully up to date, even after moving away from a desk job and getting to return to space now that the kids were old enough for Robin to handle.

That had let her send Elsy and Quinn to bed without them fretting.

Now, she was back on the verge of battle with Padraig, a position Chance honestly never expected to see. That was part of the reason she'd originally gone so far sideways with her training. Medical. Personnel. Intelligence work.

If *Wronlori* hadn't started another war, she might have been routed permanently to a staff position somewhere.

Space called her.

"Bex, give me a hard look at the backstop," Chance ordered. "Anybody sneaking up on us?"

"Not that I've been able to see on our logs, Commander," Magorian replied. "Glen and I have been running them through some astronomy software, just in case. If someone slipped past, they are too far away for us to see."

"Roger that," Chance said. "Taggart will be busy with the

new folks, so I want you to maintain both a full sphere watch as well as a conic forward, once we start to run."

"Conic?"

"There is almost no chance that Captain Boru takes the predictable route home, Bex," Chance laughed. "You've met the man. Someone parking out there will be out of position when they do figure out where we're going. Your job is to see them before they can move to intercept. Stern chase favors us, just like it did with the Leviathan."

"Even a squadron?" Doherty asked from her Gunnery station.

Kellen was aft so that *Northwind*'s Coxswain could sit forward with Maddox Nevin, if they ended up fighting.

When. No longer if. Chance had no doubts there.

"Even a squadron, Doherty," Chance answered. "Look what your boss did to prep the death ground. They might have picked it, but they left us alone too long to prepare it. Someone's about to learn a hard lesson on ancient tactics. Our job is to make sure that they can't win."

"Understood, sir," Kellen nodded.

Chance watched her boards. Halloran was nosing in faster than regulations specified, but she also had planned this. Chance had been there for the meetings with staff, where Padraig laid things out and told his people to out-think him if they could.

Several of them had risen to the challenge.

"All hands, docking imminent," Zarah called as the two airlocks got close. "Stand by to unlock secured bulkheads for passengers."

Chance nodded. By the book, if you were evacuating a ship about to flounder or explode.

Northwind was neither, but the rulebook covered this situation close enough. Open every hatch once you were certain, so that folks could move at a dead run.

Necessary today, even though everyone crossing over was a double handful of engineers. And Acting Captain Kingston, possibly about to lose her first command.

Chance knew that Padraig had ordered her to join the others. Specifically. None of that going down with your ship bullshit. Trained officers were expensive, and everything Chance had seen about Artemis Kingston said that she was exceptional.

Chance wasn't sure she could have pulled off some of those things, but she hadn't had to face that.

Chance looked around at everyone.

"Padraig and Nyssa have the line," she reminded them. "Our job is to hold the flanks for them. Given the situation, that might be more important, so stay sharp."

Nods back. Serious business.

A *Wronlori* force was about to arrive.

34

————

Padraig watched the scan. Trouble, no two ways about it, but nothing he hadn't planned for, at the end of the day.

A trio of ships approaching the system. Presumably, to land near the factory and get final instructions before attacking.

Padraig highly doubted that they were just out for a quick patrol. No, he'd fight today assuming someone had seen or heard them and expected *Marrakesh* to be a cruiser.

Thus, they'd bring trouble.

Three suggested overwhelming force, but wolfpacks were also a *Wronlori* standard tactic. Leviathans carried four, eight, or twelve, depending on the model, from standard warship, to flag command, to heavy carrier with almost no personal firepower.

He doubted that there'd be a need for a Leviathan. Not if they sent three ships. Could he get lucky and they ordered out a squadron of destroyers? *A'Zedi* called that medium-sized hull frigates, but they were roughly equivalent. Smaller than any cruiser hull and possessing commensurately shorter range. Heavy wolfpack when they traveled and fought in threes.

Cruisers, though, and he was in serious trouble, any way you sliced it. *Marrakesh* wasn't the equivalent of a single *Wronlori* cruiser, those heavy utility hulls that formed the backbone of

Wronlori's fleet. Interceptors, War Patrollers, Configurable Transports just like *Marrakesh*, or even weirder variants.

He'd have to rely on the minefield. And *Northwind* taking the brunt of the assault.

Hell of a thing, to come all this distance to rescue the ship, only to end up destroying it in the end, but he'd rescued the crew, recovered the information, and was about to be fighting for his life.

Padraig paused and considered if he should just run like hell right now, but that would likely be waving a red flag in somebody's face. He'd be back to Albany and *Sundering Wrath*, when *Marrakesh* was outclassed and trying anything to escape.

He'd gotten lucky then, and didn't really feel like pushing that sort of luck too often.

"Radio, confirm signal status to *Northwind*," he called, looking over at where Coxswain Kuchi was sitting close to Maddox.

Northwind didn't have much for particle cannons. At the same time, he wasn't about to leave the ship behind, so using it up entirely in battle was probably for the best.

How much damage could he do to the bad guys before then?

"Communications are stable and encrypted, Captain," Taggart replied.

"Arm the scuttling charges, Radio," he said, watching Kuchi flinch in spite of himself, but shrug a moment later. "Set a timer for six hours from now, then make sure you can disable the timer later if need be."

"If need be, sir?" she asked, so surprised that she turned back to look at him.

"We might win here, Radio," Padraig laughed. "I'd hate to chase those folks off, then not be able to save the ship afterwards."

She blinked, then nodded. Kuchi offered a smile, silently thanking Padraig.

"Is Konicek aboard?" he asked Nyssa.

"Aye, sir," Nyssa replied. "I confirmed her in the airlock safely."

"Helm, lock down and begin backing us away on rotary thrusters," he ordered. "Set course such that someone coming at us from the factory has to pass as close to the center of the minefield as possible. Then set *Northwind* to a parallel course, on our flank closer to the enemy on that side. I'd like to herd them a little. And make them waste fire on *Northwind,* since there's nobody over there they can hurt at present."

"Aye, sir," Zarah Halloran replied. "Course laid in and executing. *Northwind* will shadow us. Guns, you tell me what rotation you need when we have guests."

"Roger that, Helm," Maddox replied. "All gun teams, stand by. We'll start with cannon fire and missiles from both boats. Minefield comes into play once we lock them onto the death ground."

Padraig nodded at the words, citing the ancient philosopher everybody studied in school.

In difficult ground, press on; In encircled ground, devise stratagems; In death ground, fight.

This was difficult ground, deep behind enemy lines, so he'd press on as much as he could.

This was encircled ground, because he didn't have anybody nearby that he could rely on to help, while the enemy might have spent some time trying to slip a ship around behind him where they could move to intercept.

This was the death ground.

He would fight. And he had the right team in place to do it.

"Captain, Commander Kingston requests permission to join us on the bridge," Taggart said.

"Absolutely, Radio," he replied. "Bring her forward and sit her close to Kuchi where we have access to her expertise."

Padraig doubted that Artemis Kingston had seen many battles. Spy ships like hers were the quiet mice in the pantry. At least until they weren't.

Still, Kuchi would relay Padraig's words later, and she'd feel better, even if she didn't make any meaningful contributions right now.

She'd managed the damned near impossible task of holding her crew together long enough to be rescued by friends. And kept half of them alive, against the odds.

Now *Marrakesh* needed to step up and protect them. Not a warship, but his crew had seen more action than a lot of Line Cruisers did.

And in crazier situations.

The hatch opened and Artemis entered. Coxswain Kuchi waved her over and Padraig smiled.

"Glad to have you, Captain Kingston," he said, reminding her that she'd taken command, even if he was most likely about to destroy her ship.

"Thank you, Captain Boru," she replied as she slid into a seat. "What's the situation?"

"Radio, get her up to date with my feeds," Padraig said.

Some officers got prissy when they had strangers about. Didn't like to share information. Not folks Padraig liked to work with, but he knew the type. The wrong type.

This was a team effort across the board.

Padraig watched the map. Aetherial scans showed the trio drop out close to the factory.

Good. They might know where he was, but hadn't tried to drop right on top of him, so they needed a minute to update to the latest intelligence.

"All hands, this is Captain Boru," he announced on the intercom. "Enemy squadron has dropped out near the center of the station. There will be minimal warning when they launch their attack, so stand by to receive the enemy."

He closed the line and looked around.

Grim, determined faces watching their boards. Sober.

Game-face time.

He nodded.

Nothing to do now but wait.

However, he'd used the time he'd had to prepare, even as Nylund and Konicek had done everything they could to repair *Northwind*.

Not enough, but you can't win every engagement.

"All hands, squadron is in motion!" Taggart called as soon as they appeared again on her Aetherial scanners. "Contact in twenty seconds."

Padraig drew a breath and wondered how his fate would turn out.

35

Zarah watched the feed. Nyssa had added some new math or something, because suddenly a predicted flight graph appeared on it.

"Radio, are they missing us on first drop?" Zarah asked, noting that the plot was aimed precisely at where *Northwind* had been a week ago.

Before *Marrakesh* had pushed them onto a different vector.

"I think so," Nyssa replied with a shrug in her voice.

Zarah nodded, then went ahead and smiled.

"*Northwind* team, stand by to rotate," Zarah ordered. "Three-five-zero and stable. Bow up ten."

Kuchi shook his head, then turned and looked at her in confusion.

"I'll take Guns," Captain Kingston interrupted. "I see what she's doing."

"You have Guns, sir," Kuchi replied, still a little lost.

Zarah shared a smile with the woman and went back to her boards, transmitting a quick flight update to the autopilot over there.

Forward turret more centered on the probable landing point. All four point defense cannons with clear fields of fire as well.

They'd lose the ventral railgun pulsar, but better to have the particle cannons handy at this point.

"*Marrakesh*, stand by to come to heading zero-zero-five, down five," Zarah called.

Captain Boru had told her specifically that this battle was going to be all jazz until someone committed, and that she should adjust on the fly until he said something.

Thus, starboard just a hair and down a little. Move *Northwind* such that it provided an umbrella, of sorts, without actually being in the way.

A rock they could lean against and shoot over.

"CONTACT!" Nyssa called. "Three vessels. Scanning now."

Zarah noted the layout. Triangle, with the point away from her and two smaller ships forward some on the flanks.

Medium-to-long range, so they'd have to move closer to engage with the defensive particle cannon turrets, but that was normal in battle. You relied on the missiles to hurt the other guy.

Marrakesh had the two heavy twin particle turrets. *Northwind* had only one. Not a lot to engage three ships.

"Enemy squadron is two cruiser hulls and a destroyer," Nyssa called after a moment. "War Patroller, Mine Tender, Heavy Infiltrator."

"Radio, are they flying squadron colors?" Captain Boru asked.

Zarah didn't understand, but she was already flying to evade. Overhead, the big guns had already turned and started to open fire, but Maddox had known trouble was coming and planned ahead.

"*Northwind*, fire at will," he ordered. "Stand by to launch as soon as we identify our target."

Identify?

Oh. Squadron flag.

"Negative on squadron flag, sir," Nyssa replied after a moment. "Mine Tender seems to be issuing orders to the other two."

"Roger that, Radio," Captain Boru said. "Everybody beware of extreme long-range cannons on the Tender. Those probably out-range us, but lack serious punch. Ships like that use them to sweep mines from well outside the mine's normal engagement sphere. Guns, give me the first missile salvo into the War Patroller. Stand by for the reloads into the Infiltrator, once he commits to defending the squadron. This feels like they sent whoever was available in harbor when they needed to deploy the Mine Tender and knew someone had come to investigate."

Zarah focused on flying.

36

Maddox reviewed the plot. And the enemy.

Mine Tenders were usually built on cruiser hulls, in a manner similar to *Marrakesh*. Lots of space to deploy minefields. Couple of long-range guns to clear them if you needed. *Wronlori* would usually use a smaller destroyer hull to lay fields, if all they needed was an explosive curtain, so this might be the ship that had originally placed this more advanced field.

Made sense, as they'd need to place a couple more when all was said and done.

A *Wronlori* War Patroller was the equivalent of an *A'Zedi* Line Cruiser. The bigger version was an Interceptor, and could take on a battlecruiser toe to toe. Heavy Infiltrator was the standard Line Frigate back home. Decent offense. Good defense. Usually part of a trio or wolfpack, so Maddox tended to agree with the captain that this was a scratch force, thrown together for a mission without necessarily a lot of training.

How did he exploit that?

"First salvo, stand by to launch sequentially," Maddox called. "*Northwind*, your target is the War Patroller. Missile plots are being transmitted. Launch as you have them."

Two tubes on *Northwind*, one down each flank. Hardly

worth mentioning, so he'd loaded Sixes when he was aboard. Big hunks of metal in the air to distract folks, knowing that every Nine available was out in the minefield already.

Not that *Marrakesh* was much better, with three down each flank, but he didn't have three seasoned warfighters over there, either. Scratch team with the tender out of position to support the other two.

That left one sort-of heavy cruiser and a frigate to worry about.

Would the Mine Tender move up after they surveyed things? Extra defensive particle cannon could make the difference around here, but only for the stuff coming right at them. Would they even have missiles in the tubes?

Maddox turned to Nyssa.

"Radio, I need you to dig me up the specs or schematics of a *Wronlori* Mine Tender," he said simply. "Tactical question. Highest priority."

He waited for Captain Boru to override, but the man didn't say anything.

"Long range cannons, open fire on your nearest target," Maddox ordered.

Nobody was really close at this point. Smart *Wronlori* captains would sit back and put a few salvos in the air to keep *Marrakesh* and *Northwind* honest. Assuming that they didn't know any better what was going on.

Northwind was certainly acting like a warship in service, backing madly away on about a quarter power and putting fire and missiles into space.

Would it be enough to confuse them?

"Gunner, your screen five," Nyssa said a few moments later.

Maddox quickly checked, but all the gun teams were doing fine, so he could afford the distraction.

Wronlori Mine Tender.

Yeah, he'd suspected that Nyssa Taggart had access to more interesting tidbits than Maddox had been able to study. High security stuff, but he also understood that they were more in the spy business these days than line of battle patrol.

Way more interesting life, assuming you survived it.

There. Yes. Could he be that lucky?

"Radio, has the Mine Tender launched *any* missiles?" he asked, even as his defensive teams began to engage incoming shards.

Just as the *Wronlori* folks were starting to smash down the stuff he was sending at them.

You'd have to be dead lucky in order to score a hit with only eight tubes launching against a cruiser and a frigate. A War Patroller and a Heavy Infiltrator. The Mine Tender was taking potshots for now, but hadn't realized that they'd be better off shooting down missiles with that extra range, instead of trying to hurt *Northwind*.

Not yet, anyway. He'd figure it out shortly.

"Negative, Gunner," Nyssa confirmed. "No missile launches."

"Guns, what are you thinking?" Captain Boru stepped into the conversation.

"Scratch force, sir," Maddox replied. "Mine Tenders, according to Taggart's notes, usually remove the missile launchers and replace them with gear to deploy mines. Larger portals. Different hardware, mine-sized rails. No easy way to handle missiles, unless you maybe removed the shuttle bay and put a rotary launcher back there, but I'd only do that in an emergency."

"Okay, what does that gain us?" Captain Boru asked.

"Mindset, sir," Maddox replied. "They have more tubes than we do, but not enough to overwhelm us if we stay close together and let fields of fire overlap. Captain Kingston and Doherty can handle defensive fire for *Northwind*. If we stay a little closer, we might drag them by our leash. Almost have them in the kill zone, sir."

Maddox waited, but Captain didn't say anything.

"Yes," Captain finally said. "I agree. Helm, push *Northwind*'s engines past safety limits. Burn out the repairs if you have to, but back them away. Same time, let us coast some to protect *North-wind*. I'd like *Wronlori* convinced that there is a full crew fighting it and have them waste a lot of firepower on *Northwind* instead of us. Gun teams, extend your engagement spheres to protect *North-wind* from missiles. Missile teams, keep them honest. Nevin, you and Taggart trigger the minefield when you're ready."

"Aye, sir," Maddox replied. "Continuing running, retrograde engagement tactics. Got a spiderweb here. Need some flies to stumble into it."

He liked the chuckles around the bridge. According to Captain Boru, that was the sign of a loose crew. High morale.

Ready to kick ass and take names.

This was still going to get ugly before it got better.

37

Jocelyn had stripped the EVA suit off and headed aft to secondary bridge with Commander Messier. She didn't have a duty station, but Engineering would be a mess of folks keeping *Marrakesh* flying, and she might be able to help in other ways.

Messier looked up when Jocelyn entered. Then grinned when she looked at the undersuit Jocelyn was wearing. The same one that had distracted Captain Boru—and others—for the last few weeks.

"You want to handle remote engineering on *Northwind*?" Messier asked.

Jocelyn staggered to a halt, then nodded.

"I can do that," Jocelyn replied.

"Good, you take station three," Messier pointed. "Captain Boru just ordered Halloran to overload the engines and try to move the ship out of danger. You try to hold things together while we keep trouble off their back."

Jocelyn slid into the station. It was unlocked. She thought the woman next to her was named Magorian, but she'd been outside the ship more than inside while working on *Northwind*, so she wasn't sure. Couple of other females she knew only by face to date.

Quickly, she brought up readouts on *Northwind*. Squire Taggart had connected the two ships as closely as if there was a data cable running between them, instead of just comm lines. It was like she was on *Northwind*'s secondary bridge instead of *Marrakesh*'s.

"Bridge, this is Konicek," she said. "Ready to take over Engineering on *Northwind*."

"You certain, Konicek?" Captain Boru replied a moment later.

"Aye, sir," she said.

"All yours, then," he ordered. "Keep it intact as long as possible, but we're using that ship up if we have to."

"Understood, Captain."

Jocelyn checked the boards. Fuel good. Engines running a little hot, so she routed more coolant over from life support. Wasn't like she needed it elsewhere on the ship.

Then she went ahead and shut down all the blowers and the scrubbers. They could always take time to flush the bad air out of the ship later if they needed.

Every damage control bulkhead and louver got closed firmly now, and the ship was sealed up as tight as it could. A crew would be trapped in any compartment they happened to be, but there was no crew. Just folks like Jocelyn, running things remotely.

"Konicek, I show life support off," Captain Kingston came onto the line a moment later. "Is that you?"

"Affirmative, sir," Jocelyn replied. "Freeing up power for the guns and engines. Not much, but every little bit helps."

"Understood, Konicek," Kingston said. "You handle that and I'll shoot."

"Got it."

Engines were starting to cool, but that was her overloading the radiators. Anything to get more power, even as those engines hadn't been certified yet.

No time like the present, and Captain Boru had told everyone that he might have to blow the ship in place, rather than allow it to be captured.

Not if she had anything to say about it.

38

―――――

Padraig watched and listened.

He considered it the mark of a good captain that the crew were pushing the envelope without him having to kick them in the ass to get them moving.

Hell, most of the time his job seemed to be to drag on their chains to keep them from running away with themselves. Back when he was Gunner and then Executive Officer on *Nemesis*, Captain Khalil had been the same way. And had helped Padraig turn into the officer and commander he was.

He should invite the man aboard sometime, now that Khalil was retired from space duty and flying a desk. His old boss would appreciate what Padraig had here.

"Helm, bring me up a shade to cross us over," Nevin called. "*Northwind*, you're going to be pinched hard on that side with their next salvo. Stand by to put all your fire to starboard while I cover your port flank."

Padraig nodded. Maddox Nevin had spent a lot of time working out in his head how he might use this situation. And the two of them had gamed a few variations in their down time.

Time to put that to use.

Then Padraig had a thought.

"Radio, what do you read from our police cutters?" he asked.

It took Nyssa a moment, as she was tactical at this moment, scanning the three warships maneuvering to engulf *Northwind*.

"No current signal, sir," she replied. "Lag, of course, but they remain close to the factory presumably."

Padraig nodded. He noted the distances. Seven light-hours through regular space. Twenty seconds or so if you engaged Ghostdrives.

"Guns, I think I like where the two lead vessels are located," Padraig announced. "Prepare to engage with the minefield. Helm and *Northwind*, engage gyros and come about one-eight-zero on exact reciprocal course. Full thrust on rotary engines once you reverse. I want to come fully to rest as quickly as possible. Engine damage is acceptable at present, so tell Ahearn I said so."

Laughter.

Knight Jareth Ahearn took Engineering as seriously as anybody when he was working. And didn't, the rest of the time. Plus, Padraig had extra bodies who could repair things in real time.

The screens began shifting as Halloran brought them around. *Northwind* began later, but a harder turn because they didn't have crew that needed to be accounted for on the local gravity field emitters.

He wondered if any of the enemy captains would realize that *Northwind* must be uncrewed to maneuver like that.

"Guns, maximum engagement," Padraig said. "Next salvo, I want all Sixes in the tubes. Load and hold. Primary target is the cruiser, so that the frigate shifts to his flank to protect and maybe loses track of his own perimeter."

"Sixes, aye, sir," Nevin replied. "Gun teams, switch to maximum sustainable rate of fire. Damage control, stand by to fix whatever breaks without asking for permission first."

Yes. Maddox Nevin would have his own command one of these days, though Padraig would be sad to lose the man. Chance might want a ship, and she might not. They hadn't talked that much about it.

Taggart would eventually command something like *Northwind*, presumably.

Or maybe a P-class Tactical Transport, custom built to her needs.

Padraig would like to see that design. He might have a few ideas of what to add.

Then he paused and made a note to start a formal list for Madame Gelashvili. Not that she probably needed it, but he might have a few things she hadn't thought of yet.

Just like Maddox Nevin knew how to command a warship in service, Padraig's job over the next several years was making sure Nyssa Taggart did, as well.

"Helm, we are coming to rest," Halloran announced. "Enemy vessels appear to be coasting at present, but have not undergone turnover to slow down."

"As expected, Helm," Padraig agreed. "We've just done something stupid and they don't necessarily want to come to rest too close. Expect both closer vessels to turn away shortly. Guns, what is your status?"

"Radio, are we programmed as intended?" Nevin asked.

"Aye, sir," Nyssa replied. "Scenario six, with an entire hemisphere targeted on vessel two and the remainder evenly split between the other pair."

"Captain, minefield is live and ready to track," Nevin acknowledged.

Padraig waited just a shade longer, letting his scowl reach across space to that War Patroller and the Heavy Infiltrator doing an excellent job of shielding it from the few missiles *Marrakesh* had left, with *Northwind*'s tubes no longer speaking.

All of her reloads were in space around the ships, with the Mine Tender just about to cross the center of the cloud.

"Gunner, engage the minefield," Padraig ordered. "Launch all tubes as quickly as missiles clear. Gun teams, go fully defensive and stop anybody trying to score a late kill on *Northwind*."

"Aye, sir," Maddox replied, pushing a button on his console with a theatrical flourish.

Padraig leaned back and watched as his scan board suddenly came alive with signals.

War was hell. However, they'd started this war, just as they'd come to Domnall to attack him when he'd been simply trying to rescue *Northwind* from internment.

Or something worse.

Around him, hell erupted.

39

Nyssa had worked with Zarah to plot a whole series of scenarios, once Maddox had laid out how he thought it would all go down. And how many ships might be coming.

Scenario Six had presumed a squadron of three vessels, as had indeed occurred. Maddox had specified that he wanted the squadron commander to face most of the thirty missiles when they tracked, so she'd sliced the sphere into four parts and sent two of them after the War Patroller.

Sixes and Nines, because *Northwind*'s first salvo had been the only two Threes they had in inventory, followed by a pair of Sixes that hadn't done anything except give the *Wronlori* gun teams live fire practice.

Missiles lurking in the darkness came to life with anti-matter fire suddenly thrusting them into motion. Slow acceleration, but the range was sufficient to get them going fast enough to be trouble.

Then they would split into six or nine parts on ballistic arcs, because at that speed, even nuclear weapons didn't add much to the energy of a ton of steel impacting something. Plus, the steel would penetrate like a bullet, instead of merely exploding on the surface.

Nyssa had turned on all of her scanners to maximum emissions, both to confuse the enemy warships as well as to provide Maddox's missiles the most accurate targeting data they could get as they lined up and lit up.

In a few seconds, the sky was filled with shooting stars, then the three enemy ships were suddenly firing every which way, trying to defend themselves from enough arrows to shadow the sun, as the ancients had once said.

And both *Northwind* and *Marrakesh* were drawing closer as well.

It was enough to make an enemy captain made mistakes. Captain Boru had explained such a thing. And she'd seen it at Albany, against *Sundering Wrath*.

You could be the best captain with the best crew in the galaxy, but the other guy *might just get lucky...*

The Mine Tender hadn't been paying attention to his own rear flank. A Nine back there overwhelmed his suddenly panicked gunners. A shard got through and struck the ship a glancing blow that backlit it like the dawn on her visual cameras. Then it began tumbling, a victim of physics.

The Heavy Infiltrator was a combat-oriented escort, so it did the best job at engaging various missile fragments, but the captain had obviously been ordered to protect the War Patroller, because it didn't put all of its own defensive fire where it should have.

Nyssa remembered the hit that had so badly damaged *Sundering Wrath*. This was more like one of the wolfpack ships that had taken a shard right through the center of the ship.

It flashed like a supernova. When that first burst of terrible light cleared, the ship had broken into two pieces, almost alike in size, headed in different directions.

That left the cruiser. It had many guns. And good crews. They killed one fragment after another, and might have gotten them all, had they only faced a quarter of the mass, instead of half of it.

And *Northwind*'s guns, under Captain Kingston's command,

had centered their heavy particle cannons on the ship and over-loaded. Had actually flashed warnings all over her board when something broke. Possibly a coolant line, but Nyssa would have to review the logs to know and it didn't matter right now.

What mattered was that Kingston had tattooed that ship's hull with several bolts. Maybe only shattering the armored skin and not penetrating, but something got through, because the nearest flank of the ship went dark for several seconds as she watched.

While missile fragments closed at one percent of light speed.

Impact.

She'd heard that it was actually almost impossible to cause a warship to explode. They were built too tough. Too many durable bulkheads and frames designed to survive. Fuel systems and missile storage compartments were built to vent an explosion away from the ship, sacrificing a chunk of the hull for the safety of the rest of the crew.

One of the missile fragments entered the vessel almost perfectly in the center of the ship's cylinder, passing forward through Engineering. Then right up the ship's spine, when Nyssa went back and reviewed her logs in ultra-slow motion.

It came apart. Simply shattered into a thousand smaller pieces, no longer recognizable as a starship.

"Captain, all enemy vessels are off-line," she announced as something of a stunned anti-climax.

It had taken nine seconds, according to the clock on her console.

And the enemy squadron had ceased to exist.

Now what?

40

Padraig was aghast. Shocked almost beyond words, watching the corona of flaming gases cool that had been a *Wronlori* War Patroller all of sixty seconds ago.

Gone.

The Infiltrator was broken into two pieces. The Mine Tender was tumbling on three axes and didn't have any external lights running at present.

"Radio, what's the Mine Tender's status?" he asked.

"Your screen nine, sir," Taggart said.

Padraig checked. Stern hit. High, where the ventral railgun had been blind and the dorsal had been aiming forward.

Because nobody had expected an envelopment.

He drew a breath and triggered the comm.

"Flight deck, get both birds in the air immediately for rescue operations," he ordered. "Radio will route you to sailors that survived and are floating in space. Medical and Security, stand by to assist, once we know what we've got."

He cut that line and turned to Nyssa.

"Get me the Mine Tender's captain on the comm," Padraig said. "Demand his immediate surrender and ransom to assist if they can. Otherwise, have him shut everything down and behave so I don't have to destroy him to make my point. Am I clear?"

"Aye, sir," she said with big eyes.

He knew he could trust Nyssa Taggart to convey what he needed.

He keyed a number.

"Secondary Bridge. Magorian."

"Bex, Nyssa is busy local," he continued. "Make sure those six police cutters don't get frisky. If they move, sound the alarm and route targeting information to the Gunner, because we'll kill them as soon as they land."

"Aye, sir," Magorian replied.

"Gunner, stand by to unleash hell if anybody gives me any reason," Padraig turned to Nevin. "If any ship fires on us, destroy all of them. That is a direct order, sailor."

"Sir. Yes, sir," Maddox nodded.

Formal orders like that would mean that Padraig got yelled at later, rather than Maddox Nevin, but if the Mine Tender still wanted to get stupid, there would be shuttles and friendlies he could hurt.

That was not allowed.

Padraig reviewed things in his head as his crew worked. Then he dialed a number.

"Secondary bridge. Konicek."

"Knight, two questions," Padraig replied. "One, is it worth putting you and your folks EVA to help rescue sailors? Two, what is the status of *Northwind* as a warship in service?"

"EVA probably doesn't help much immediately, Captain," she said. "We don't have the thrusters to chase someone down on a bad vector like a shuttle does. I'd suggest docking with *Northwind* and dropping a full repair crew aboard. My notes here from Walker suggest that we might be able to jury-rig the Ghostdrives enough to get a safer distance away."

"What's safer?" he asked.

"Several light-years, but it will be slowly," she replied. "Mark

Two, probably. Still nobody around but the cutters. How soon will they come to investigate?"

Padraig nodded.

That was the exact question that everything else hinged on. The light from this battle would be visible deeper in the system in six to eight hours, depending on where folks were orbiting.

Would the cutters decide to attack at that point? Or would they see the cruisers being annihilated and decide that they needed to remain defensive around the factory?

And was that courage or cowardice?

Would they come in the short term, a second wave intended to surprise *Marrakesh* in the middle of a battle?

This one had ended far quicker than normal. Twenty-one minutes of terror packed down tight, instead of hours of maneuvering and lobbing missiles back and forth like you got when war squadrons engaged.

And every decision he might make right now was fraught with risk.

Padraig turned to Coxswain Kuchi and Captain Kingston.

"Captain Kingston, I'd like to save your ship, if possible," he said simply. "If the cutters come, you risk capture again."

"Acceptable, Captain," Artemis nodded. "Like you, I'd like to bring her home."

"Konicek, stand by to put teams onto *Northwind* as soon as we can dock," he said. "Then you and Captain Kingston will immediately withdraw from the battlefield at high speed until you can transition to Ghost-space or determine that to be an impossible task. Radio, you work it out with Helm as we start collecting stray kittens. Move it people."

Nyssa was hunched over her console, talking forcefully, but gave him a thumbs up.

"No, I don't care, *Ellsworth*," Nyssa snarled angrily. "You will surrender to ransom right now or we will destroy you without mercy. Those are Captain Boru's terms. Do you wish to die?"

Padraig started to say something, but caught himself short.

Harsh, but effective. And she sounded decades older than she really was. Like Kaitlin Lynch having an exceptionally bad day.

There had been a few. Thankfully, none of them his fault.

"Understood, *Ellsworth*," she continued a moment later, listening to an earpiece. "You will take actions to kill your spin and stabilize the vessel. Anything else will be considered a hostile act and dealt with accordingly. We will begin delivering to your vessel wounded and rescued *Wronlori* sailors, so clear your flight deck. Preferably by getting your shuttles into motion to assist us. They will take my orders on this channel. Out."

Padraig grinned. Nyssa Taggart was going to be one hell of a captain, one of these days, striding her own deck like a titan if she decided that was the path for her.

His job was to make it possible for her.

Aftermath, every direction he looked, but Padraig Boru had a sharp crew.

And they'd manufactured their own luck today.

<h1 style="text-align:center">41</h1>

Jocelyn was first across the threshold onto *Northwind*. She'd paused to throw on a jacket, mostly for the pockets, but otherwise was in her EVA undersuit, ignoring the snide commentary from the men and women in the airlock with her.

They were all just jealous of her body.

Into the first corridor and turn right. She'd brought life support back on once the shooting had stopped, and it hadn't had long enough to get stale or cold over here, so she was jogging.

"Ryan, you and Martinez get the Ghostdrive open for inspection immediately," she called as a dozen folks pounded after her down the hallway. "I'll inspect engines, but we know that they passed today's test and I'm willing to push them a little. Everybody else, to your stations and make sure nothing is leaking, burning, or broken, with really low standards for acceptable, if it gets us out of here."

"How long do we have, boss?" Ryan asked as he jogged in her wake, a toolbox thumping against one thigh with every other step.

"I need to know if it's impossible in twenty minutes," Jocelyn replied. "Then, how long you think it will take. We have five hours until the locals see the light-speed wave and know what happened, assuming they are paying attention. In that time, we need to be gone, one way or the other."

"Roger that," he said, and fell silent.

The jog wasn't long. *Marrakesh* had put them at the aft airlock, since that was where most of the work would be happening.

Engineering hadn't changed much from the last time she'd walked in here. Both holes were covered over and sealed, the one on the floor showing a lot of foot traffic.

Some mook had painted a happy face bullseye on the plate where the beam had entered, but it hadn't been worth tearing a kilo of flesh off someone then.

Jocelyn still intended to sand it off herself at some point. Or paint it over with standard hull gray.

There were limits to what the crew could be expected to find funny, especially given how many folks had been killed in here.

Warm bodies went every which way as they entered.

Jocelyn had a power torque in one hand already and backed bolts out over the main fuel feed as soon as she confirmed that it wasn't holding in any dangerous gases. Bad time to flash burst something in her face.

Innards looked solid. Jocelyn put the torque down and grabbed a tester rig from a pocket, connecting wires and reading results far faster than she would have allowed anybody else to do it.

At least in any other situation.

Today was an extra bit of special.

Her comm beeped in a pocket. She pulled it out and juggled things around, then put it on the case and kept working.

"Konicek."

"How are the engines looking?" Captain Kingston asked simply. "My boards all read green."

"Same here, sir," Jocelyn said. "I think you can bring things up to maybe twenty percent without any risk. Then we'll watch and see."

"Excellent news, Konicek," Kingston said with a smile in her voice. "Stand by for power."

"Everybody, engines are turning on!" she leaned back and yelled through the space.

Those three big generators were all humming happily, with the fourth a total loss that would either need to be dismantled in place or removed once the ship was in dry-dock and folks could take off hull plates carefully sometime later.

Hands waved acknowledgment as heads were down inside things eyeballing equipment and repairs. She had a good team.

The fuel feed started to hum as the engines lit. Everything had already been pushed, but Jocelyn had been watching from *Marrakesh* during the battle and adjusting things there. No leaks or breaks then or since meant that she had a higher comfort level, at least for this part.

She leaned back and looked around. Assholes and elbows, because everybody was working. Bent over, squatting down, heads in compartments, something.

The lights flickered twice, then the generators caught up and started delivering more power. Jocelyn made a note to check feeds. Might have a wire close to shorting, but the beasts were delivering the juice that *Northwind* needed right now.

That was more than she could have hoped for an hour ago. Or a day ago.

Leaving her testing rig attached, she moved over to where Ryan and Martinez were working. Plates off. Ryan handing the other man tools and spare parts in a nearly silent ballet.

She waited. Ryan shrugged. Martinez never looked up once.

"Power torque," Martinez asked, hand back.

Ryan handed it to him.

Martinez cinched down a pair of bolts, then leaned back and studied the mess. He leaned in and torqued something.

He turned to her.

"Got a ducat says it burns out before we travel ten light-years in this condition," he said solemnly. "Tell the Captain to pick a closer target so I can get back in here and rewire a chunk of stuff that would have been next on my list tomorrow anyway."

Jocelyn nodded. There was a reason this man was on point today. She grabbed her comm.

"Kingston," the woman answered.

"My folks say eight light-years is pushing it for current repairs," Jocelyn told her. "Do you have a rendezvous we can hit in that sphere?"

"Affirmative, Knight," Kingston replied. "Stand by to bring everything live, then tell me when you are ready to engage Ghostdrives."

"Roger that, Captain," Jocelyn said, cutting the line. "All hands, we are go for Ghost. Make sure whatever you're doing will hold, then give me a positive signal."

She waited, then slowly turned in place, getting waves, nods, or something from everybody or every team. Finally, she circled back to Martinez.

"Your call," she said simply.

"Here goes nothing," he said, reaching for the rocker switch he'd added in at some point and flipping it.

The generators got louder. And came up a minor third on the scale. Nothing broke, exploded, or caught fire. About as good as today was getting, even if all the particle cannon fire had been on the armor and outer hull.

Northwind was an ugly mess, but nothing a few weeks in dry-dock couldn't fix with a facelift, some paint, and a few new panels here and there.

Martinez counted to ten and nodded at her.

"How fast, you think?" she asked him.

Martinez turned to Mathias Ryan.

"Mark Two point Five oughta be safe, if they come up slowly from One point Five," Ryan said. "Slowly is the key here."

Jocelyn nodded. The transition to Ghost-space was always a bit jarring, but the slower you entered, the less impact on fragile systems. Useful, when you were fragile.

Not always possible on a warship.

"Kingston," the captain answered immediately.

"We're ready here, Captain," Jocelyn told her. "Slow in insertion, then bring it up slowly to Two point Oh until we see how it holds. We might be able to eke out more."

"Thank you, Konicek," the woman said. "And thank your people. I truly doubt you understand how much your work means to my crew, so let me speak for all of them."

"We're getting you home, sir," Jocelyn said. "That's what we do."

42

———

Padraig had a symphony going in his head. Even in suits, there were few survivors that had made it off the War Patroller alive. Lots of dead men and women in suits that had been prioritized last, once Nyssa had scanned their life settings.

The Infiltrator had broken in two, with both pieces relatively intact, just headed in different directions. The stern had some power, while the bow had batteries sufficient to handle life support for now.

The Mine Tender *Ellsworth* had come to rest, more or less. Still drifting through space, but not under power and providing a central point from which five shuttles had been able to birddog sailors on their lonely way into the cold darkness.

And *Ellsworth*'s captain hadn't had anything to say about *Marrakesh*'s shuttles docking to drop off people before leaving immediately. Padraig hadn't even put more than one security crew member on each, providing more space for folks in life suits to hop out and grab folks, then pull them inside to safety.

There were worse ways to die in service, but Padraig was willing to move heaven and earth right now so that none of these men and women had to face that death.

Not today. Not on his watch.

His comm chimed.

"Bridge. Boru," he replied.

"This is Captain Kingston," Artemis said. "We're ready to test the Ghostdrives, Padraig. I've transmitted our intended flight path to Squire Taggart in case something breaks and you need to find us."

"That's fantastic news, Captain," Padraig replied. "Looking forward to sailing into harbor with you in a few weeks. Do you need anything else from us at present?"

"Negative, Captain," Artemis said. "See you on the far side."

He turned and watched as *Northwind* disappeared from his local screen and appeared on the Aetherial scanners, racing slowly away as it ran for a quiet spot outside of scanner range.

Padraig let his smile encompass the entire bridge crew. They'd been on duty all day, busting their asses, but this was what victory looked like, not defeat.

He keyed the comm.

"All hands, stand by for combat operations," he announced calmly. "*Northwind* has departed, and I expect our police cutter friends to suddenly come over to see what just happened. Flight deck, retrieve your birds immediately. If they have rescued sailors, make sure that they are dropped with emergency beacons on for one of the others to pick up. We are not staying long."

He cut the line and went back to his symphony, wondering if he'd guessed wrong.

He didn't have to wait for long.

"RADIO! Wolfpack inbound," Nyssa yelled. "Three vessels in formation. Ten seconds to contact."

"Gunner, hold fire until I order," Padraig said sharply. "Helm, once the shuttles are aboard, back us away. Engineering, stand by for Ghostdrives."

Contact. Three new blips moved from the Aetherial scanners to local. Police cutters, but he was willing to bet that they had much bigger particle cannons than ships that small should have.

Range was medium, because they'd come out knowing where *Northwind* had gone in.

"Radio, open me a hailing frequency," Padraig ordered. "Make sure that *Ellsworth* is listening, but I don't care if the captain is available or not."

"Hailing open, sir," Nyssa said immediately.

"Attention *Wronlori* squadron," Padraig said in a stern, cold voice. "This is currently a rescue operation. Stand down from combat or withdraw. Reply on this frequency."

"They're setting up an encrypted channel to Mine Tender *Ellsworth*, sir," Nyssa said quietly. "Should I try to crack it?"

"Yes, but only say something if they order an attack," he replied. "I hope they look at what happened and rethink any belligerency."

"*DC Marrakesh*, this is *Police Cutter F739*," a woman's voice came over the line. "What do you mean, rescue operation?"

"Two of your ships have been destroyed, *F739*," Padraig replied. "Mine Tender *Ellsworth* has been badly damaged by my forces. We have been rescuing your sailors and putting them aboard *Ellsworth*. You are welcome to assist. In fact, now that you are here, I intend to withdraw to allow you to complete those operations, coordinating with *Ellsworth*. That is, unless you felt the need to escalate hostilities?"

He let that hang out there. Three upgunned cutters were more than a match for *Marrakesh*, but they wouldn't know that.

What they would see would be one cruiser than had somehow blown up a *Wronlori* War Patroller, broken a Heavy Infiltrator, and badly damaged a Mine Tender.

A smart commander would explore other options right now.

Every encounter didn't have to be to the death, did it?

He waited, eyes on Maddox Nevin as they both prepared to unleash hell.

If necessary.

Padraig would prefer to live in a world where that wasn't usual.

The wait dragged. Probably the four *Wronlori* commanders arguing on a different channel, but Taggart didn't make any sudden signals, so he watched.

"*DC Marrakesh*, you are withdrawing?" the woman finally asked.

Padraig turned to Zarah Halloran. Got her signal that *Flight of Fancy* was docked.

"That's correct, *F739*," he said. "I would appreciate you not pursuing, as we've rescued our own ship and will be escorting it home. You have your own people to take care of."

More pause. Nevin was poised. Padraig watched all his people tense.

"Safe sailing, *Marrakesh*," the woman said.

Padraig blew out a heavy, silent breath and cut the line.

"Helm, take us home," he ordered.

43

Padraig watched the scene from a wide transsteel window on the top of the Forward Repair Depot, where towers had extended upward, then sent octopus tentacles every which way around *Northwind* like a giant hug.

It was that, or a predator scarfing down a meal. He preferred the friendlier image.

If you didn't need a planet to orbit, any space in the darkness was as good as any other, so he'd let Zarah and Nyssa find them a spot well away from any solar system where somebody might be lurking, prospecting, or hiding out from the law. Inside that zone that both sides claimed, so he was on stronger legal ground, if it came down to technical minutiae.

Northwind still looked horrible. One dueling scar plus one bullet wound, with a variety of slashes from the more recent battle, carving up the armor and venting outer chambers, but these ships were designed with nothing important along that outer edge, for that reason. Storage and personnel quarters for the most part, presuming that crew would be at action stations deeper inside in a battle.

Repairs were proceeding nicely. Walker Nylund was in charge

again, at least until something appeared on an Aetherial scanner, but Taggart's people were keeping a round-the-clock watch, with orders to immediately bring the ship to alert if they saw anybody.

They'd been alone for a week now.

Padraig was watching figures move in a complicated ballet of EVA, riding thruster backpacks as they maneuvered a few exterior plates around and replaced damaged equipment. Things were less frenetic than they had been before, but Konicek and her folks still moved with sure quickness.

No wasted motions at all. Detach something, either by removing bolts or cutting away damage. Carry it to a handy skiff and hook it under the cargo net. Grab the new pieces and maneuver them delicately into place.

Wouldn't be pretty, but Padraig didn't think that anything less than six months in dry-dock would do that.

He was happier to get *Northwind* and its crew home, though he did occasionally stop to wonder what sort of reputation *Marrakesh* might be building with *Wronlori* folks. *Sundering Wrath*, Monsanch, Varfelis Station, and now Domnall.

Somebody had a file on his ship. And probably him. Hopefully, Madame Gelashvili would take that into account, and they could have a few quiet runs for a time. Let things calm down, without *Marrakesh* deep in the middle of trouble.

Not that he believed it, but it made for a nice wish.

For now, he watched one figure finish mounting a new sensor array nearby and bolt everything down. Padraig didn't think she had seen him standing here, but she rotated in place when she was done and waddled slowly over to the portal, the two of them separated by about a meter.

Her faceplate was mirrored, so he had no idea what expression she had on her face right now. Honestly, he wasn't seeing her in that suit, anyway, but down to the skin-tight outfit she'd been wearing. And the smile.

He held out a hand, placing it against the transsteel from his side. A moment later, she did the same from the vacuum of space.

If the reports were still on track, *Northwind* would be ready to limp home with her remaining crew, plus folks from the Forward Repair Depot and a handful of *Marrakesh*'s engineers.

It would be a slow jaunt.

Padraig was looking forward to taking a little personal time.

44

———

Nyssa hadn't thought that she would ever get used to it, let along blasé, but she had. Comfortable, even, sitting in the waiting lounge of the *A'Zedi* Intelligence Services main bureau.

The benches were hard wood, polished by generations of uniformed bottoms. The tile was old and showed indications that it had been hand painted, about one tile in five across the floor and waist-high on the walls. Mostly *A'Zedi* mulberry, mauve, and white, so she kind of faded into it if she stopped moving.

Beside her, Captain Boru was also in his best uniform, though neither of them had the dress medals you were normally expected to wear when dressed like this in public.

Because they weren't in a navy office where it mattered. The folks behind the counter wore brown or blue for the most part. Civilians/ You would not mistake them for sailors. Older, as well, well into middle age generally, with an air of composed sternness that hardly ever smiled. They kept reminding her of her dad in many ways.

Nyssa kept herself serious. Madame Gelashvili had summoned them quietly, once *Marrakesh* had gotten back to Horwin, after depositing *Northwind* and the Forward Repair Depot at *Eworn*, where this war had started five years ago.

They were the only folks on this side of the counter. Captain Boru had made sure that they arrived ten minutes before the scheduled time, and it had been seventeen minutes sitting.

Madame Gelashvili appeared at the door herself, dressed in a more formal outfit than Nyssa had seen on her before, the few times she had been here.

"Captain Boru?" the woman called. "Squire Taggart? Could you join me, please?"

Nyssa was up even quicker than the captain, and followed him to the end of the aisle. Or pew. Through a half-door separating the bureaucrats from the sailors, though the locals nodded and didn't look so unfriendly now.

Into a hallway and back past several closed doors marked only by numbers. No names.

Operational Security, built into the DNA of the office itself. Nyssa had learned far more about those sorts of things than she'd imagined, even a year ago.

Madame Gelashvili's office had not changed. Vast expanse of wood for a desk. Two comfortable chairs that she and the captain stood behind as the Permanent First Secretary got settled behind the desk.

"Sit, please," she gestured. "Taggart, get the door."

Nyssa sat and then reached back with a hand, closing them in.

The Secretary looked stern for a moment, then her face broke into a huge grin.

"Captain Boru, there are various Marshals of different ranks who would like to be utterly cross with you," she chuckled. "However, my experts have pointed out that none of them could have come up with a better response to the situation. Plus, several of the old salts, including retired ones who advise my office, were grateful that you took the time to rescue forty-three sailors from what might have been their deaths, over and above *Northwind*'s crew. There will be a ship commendation added quietly to your file, plus a medal for you, Captain."

"Thank you, ma'am," he said. "Trying to do my duty as older officers trained me to see it."

"I wish more officers had your mindset, Boru," she nodded. "Too many of them have been institutionalized by the navy to only see things one way. All that propaganda has gone to their heads and they forget that *Wronlori* is only a political enemy. Not a personal one."

Nyssa watched him nod, but remain silent. Madame Gelashvili turned to eyeball her next. Nyssa tried to sit perfectly still, calmly watching the woman back.

"Squire, you have performed at a higher level of skill and professionalism than even the original estimations in your file," the Secretary began. "Now, having seen *Northwind* at close quarters, what are your thoughts on that aspect of the fleet, for your future career?"

"Ma'am?" Nyssa asked, confused.

"She's asking if you wanted to consider permanently moving into spy ships that do dedicated surveillance work, like *Northwind*," Captain Boru explained.

"Oh…" Nyssa finally understood.

Nyssa considered it. She'd had a chance to work closely with Captain Kingston on that aspect of things, making sure all of her data was safely recovered. At the same time, what had happened to *Northwind* was an extreme case.

According to Kingston, those ships normally went their entire sailing careers, possibly more than one generation, never encountering hostilities of any kind. Slip into the edge of a system. Park quietly and watch, if nobody saw them arrive, then race madly away if they did.

Nyssa wouldn't say she enjoyed the chaos and noise of starship combat, but she understood that the adventures that *Marrakesh* would be sent on would be so much different.

Broader, if anything. Sailing to places like Monsanch or Varfelis. And they still hauled cargo pods and other things between *A'Zedi* naval bases, so she got to see all sides of things.

"Permission to speak freely, sir?" she asked, aware that anything she said would still be written down and possibly used against her later.

But she wanted to be frank, if possible.

"Granted, Taggart," the Secretary replied. "What's on your mind?"

"I think I'd be more effective on *Marrakesh*, sir," Nyssa said, wrapping her mind around the words and feeling comfortable with them.

"And later?" the woman asked.

"Later, I think that your organization ought to consider building a few more ships like *Marrakesh*, sir," Nyssa said. "Support ships, and thus generally overlooked, but capable of undertaking certain operations without rousing suspicion."

"Interesting," Gelashvili replied. "And that might entice you to stay in uniform, Squire?"

Oh? OH!

They thought that Nyssa might hit the end of her six-year enlistment period and go back to being a civilian?

It made a certain bit of sense, when she considered it. Captain Boru and the other officers had all gone to university to learn how to be officers, and thus the fleet had had several years to mold and understand them.

Nyssa Taggart was a wildcard. An enlisted sailor promoted directly to officer, instead of getting that option after ten or twenty years in uniform.

And she had an entire career ahead of her, if she was reading these two correctly.

Did she want that? Did she want to turn into Captain Boru in another fifteen or twenty years? On the one hand, folks had mentioned how exceptional Boru was as a commanding officer. And she had other officers she worked with who were also friendly and helpful. She'd originally been concerned about how she would fit in.

To make it a career? And as a sailor, instead of sitting comfortably in an office, reviewing all the data someone else had gathered, off having adventures?

Nyssa wasn't entirely sure, but she also didn't need to be today.

"I enjoy what I do, sir," she said, eyes locked with the Secretary. "And look forward to being able to continue it. Captain Boru has a fantastic team."

"He does, Squire," the woman nodded. "We've had some concerns that normal attrition and naval operations would force us to lose some folks, as they got promoted and were no longer available in certain billets. At the same time, the entire navy is younger than it might have been, a result of opening up enlistment when the most recent war broke out, so there is less pressure. If people are happy at what they do."

Nyssa nodded. Considered her words.

She turned to Captain Boru.

"How soon until we might lose Maddox Nevin?" Nyssa asked.

He nodded.

"That one is in line to get his own boat at some point," Captain Boru replied. "Possibly soon, if he wanted to transfer over as Executive Officer on a frigate. Certainly within a few years, depending. I haven't asked him directly what his intended career path looks like. Certainly, mine didn't involve my own command this quickly, but as she said, the fleet is running young right now, and we have options."

"You will have quiet chats with all of your officers, Captain," the Secretary ordered in a nice voice. "Chance Messier is also an interesting case, given the wide range of things she did while deskbound as her children were young. And Stevedore Lynch might retire entirely if this crew changed significantly. Find out what would make all of them happy enough to stay in place. I like what you've been able to do thus far, and look forward to other things that a vessel and crew like *Marrakesh* might accomplish for me. Past that, you've just had a major mission, and *Marrakesh* will need to be inspected, in spite of what Walker Nylund said in his reports about making the ship better than it was when he boarded, so your crew should all be cycled through liberty for the next few weeks. Questions?"

"None presently, sir," Captain Boru replied. "That may change as I research things, but they all understand that we have something special here, and I don't think most of them want to change it. At least not yet. Given another year, that might change."

"Yes, it might," the Secretary nodded. "Buy me that year, Boru. And you, Taggart. Dismissed."

"Thank you, sir," Nyssa said as she rose.

They got into the hallway quickly, then out of the building entirely. Horwin's capital city of Roydon was having a fantastically perfect day. Cool weather and clear skies.

Nyssa found herself standing next to Captain Boru on a paved square, right at that point where governmental and naval offices and buildings transitioned to civilian.

She felt poised, but indecisive.

"I don't know what to do, sir," she finally said as he patiently watched.

"Then don't do anything," he replied.

"Sir?"

"If nothing demands that you act, you don't have to," he said. "Madame Gelashvili has given us a reprieve to find what we can do. I want you to do the same. Find that thing that will bring you joy."

"Could I shave my head entirely, sir?" Nyssa asked, pushing just a bit. "Keep it shaved like you do your whiskers?"

"If that's what it takes," he grinned. "I'll enter a general order when we get back to the ship."

She smiled and started walking. It wasn't everything, but it was a start.

What did she want to do with the rest of her life?

READ MORE

Be sure to read the rest of the Operation Marrakesh series!

https://www.knottedroadpress.com/product-category/science-fiction/operation-marrakesh

ABOUT THE AUTHOR

Blaze Ward writes science fiction in the Alexandria Station universe (Jessica Keller, The Science Officer, The Story Road, etc.) as well as several other science fiction universes, such as Star Dragon, the Dominion, and more. He also writes odd bits of high fantasy with swords and orcs. In addition, he is the Editor and Publisher of *Boundary Shock Quarterly Magazine*. You can find out more at his website www.blazeward.com, as well as Facebook, Goodreads, and other places.

Blaze's works are available as ebooks, paper, and audio, and can be found at a variety of online vendors. His newsletter comes out regularly, and you can also follow his blog on his website. He really enjoys interacting with fans, and looks forward to any and all questions—even ones about his books!

Never miss a release!
If you'd like to be notified of new releases, sign up for my newsletter.

http://www.blazeward.com/newsletter/

Buy More!
Did you know that you can buy directly from the KRP website?

https://www.knottedroadpress.com/shop/

Connect with Blaze!

Web: www.blazeward.com
Boundary Shock Quarterly (BSQ):
https://www.boundaryshockquarterly.com/

ABOUT KNOTTED ROAD PRESS

Knotted Road Press publishes dynamic fiction set in exotic locations and unique non-fiction voices in genres such as autobiography, business, cookbooks, and how-to. Our authors cover a wide range of genres including science fiction, fantasy, mystery, literary, and poetry, appealing to all readers. We offer both DRM-free ebooks and print books for a global readership.

Knotted Road Press
www.KnottedRoadPress.com
www.KnottedRoadPress.com/Shop